Tooth and Claw
by
Leigh Dovey

Tooth and Claw

Leigh Dovey

Published by Leigh Dovey, 2024.

CHAPTER ONE

Ben's eyes snapped open. They were wide and alert, quickly swiveling around, scanning the here and now for information. His ears picked out *Beck* on the Camper van stereo, as his brain worked to filter dream from reality and past from present. His anxiety began to subside. He felt burning. His eyes dropped to his trembling right hand. A smoking roll-up had burned down to the filter between his fingers and left dead ash on the back of his hand. He reached over and took the cigarette and stubbed it out in the dashboard's ashtray. He then covered his shaking hand, holding it steady until the tremors subsided.

Ben looked over at the woman on his right. A scruffy, beautiful blonde looked back at him from behind the wheel of the Camper van and smiled. She then turned her attention back to the empty stretch of road ahead of them. Ben reached down between his legs and retrieved a bottle of water. He took a long swig and then splashed some on to his hot face. He flipped down his sunscreen and stared at himself in the mirror. His dark hair was long and unkempt, and his skin heavily tanned by the Australian sun, except for the white patches of old scar tissue running down the left side of his forehead and cheek. He looked every one of his tired thirty-five years, and then some. The real giveaway was the eyes. Dark and haunted; they'd just seen too much.

Ben adjusted the sunscreen's mirror to reveal a perpetual, empty road stretching into the distance behind them. He sighed and switched his gaze back to the horizon ahead. He stared at the endless road playing out before them. There was nothing else to see, until he noticed a distant, lone white speck travelling towards them.

Ben offered Jo the water bottle and she took it. He lowered the passenger window and leaned out, letting the rush of air cool his face. He surveyed the vast expanse of dry scrub stretching out towards the waters of The Great Australian Bight. The scene was one of beautiful desolation beneath a grey, foreboding sky. He stared absently through a bent and broken car bumper lying in the dust by the side of the road as they passed by.

His mind was still on the dream. The same dream he always had when he closed his eyes; the one where he lost control of his Audi, while switching lanes recklessly. The one where the car buckled and twisted, as screeching metal folded in on them and shattered glass filled the air. The one where he lost Rebecca.

"You, OK?" said Jo.

Ben nodded without taking his eyes off the road.

"How far?" he said.

"You don't want to know," said Jo. "We should've gone to Cairns."

"Nah, it's a tourist trap. Too many drunken backpackers throwing up.

"You mean too much sun and fun."

Ben stared past Jo. Behind her the vast nothingness of the dry and faded plains of the interior reached as far as the eye could see. He looked out through the windscreen again. The approaching vehicle shimmered against the road in the distance. It was still too far away to see properly; perhaps it was even a mirage.

"That's the first one today," said Jo.

"Oh really?"

"Yeah Mr.Sarccy. It's your turn to wave."

"You do it, it's stupid."

"That's the point," said Jo, "Strangers, the middle of nowhere. Go on lighten up, be stupid."

Ben rolled his eyes and then a cigarette. Jo took a deep breath and held her temper. She was trying, but she'd had her fill of his moods on this trip.

"I wonder where they're going," she said.

"East."

Jo glared at him and held it this time, waiting for eye contact. Ben just exhaled smoke and stared straight ahead to avoid any confrontation.

The approaching vehicle was clearly visible now. It was an old white freezer van, its bodywork scuffed and marked. Ben craned to try and see the driver, but the cab's interior was too dark. The dusty paintwork on the van's hide was scraped and scarred, and its bull-bars were cracked and bent from numerous impacts. Ben began to tab on his roll-up nervously.

"We're doing this trip for you, you know," said Jo. "For us, but if you're going to keep digging at me…"

Ben instinctively leaned back in his seat, bracing himself, his eyes wide again. The approaching van began swerving violently one way, then another, invading their lane, crossing back, and then invading it again. Ben jabbed a finger, pointing dead ahead.

"Shit," said Jo. "What's he doing?"

Ben didn't answer; he couldn't, he was frozen with fear. Again, the van steered out into their lane, but this time it remained there. Its bull-bars beared down on them as it came straight towards them. Jo hauled on the steering wheel and the Camper van slid off the road, narrowly missing the other vehicle. The Camper van's wheels locked, as it tilted and skied through the dirt towards a gulley running alongside the road, churning up a cloud of thick, brown dust. The passenger side of the Camper van crunched to a halt against the wall of the roadside trench. Ben's window shattered and erupted into a shower of glistening shards. The Camper van's bodywork groaned as the impact travelled through the rest of the vehicle.

The sand and dust slowly settled, revealing the creased Camper van intact, but wedged tightly into the ditch at the side of the road. The freezer van that forced them there was nowhere to be seen.

Ben's eyes flickered beneath their lids and then opened. He looked across at Jo slumped next to him, held fast by her seat belt. He reached over and squeezed her shoulder. She groaned in reply. Ben closed his eyes and whispered a small "thank you" to someone up there. He unclipped his safety belt, then reached across and released her. He supported Jo's weight as she flopped down against him. She started to come around.

"You OK baby?" he said.

Jo took a deep breath and sighed, as she opened her dazed eyes. It was a few moments before they could find focus, then she smiled at him.

"I think so," she said. "You?"

"Yeah," he said. "I'm fine now."

Ben ran his fingers through her hair.

"I thought I'd lost you." he said.

"No such luck Mister."

Jo leaned away and sat up, groaning.

"So much for the road trip therapy," she said.

"That idiot must have been drunk," said Ben. "The way he was swerving...what?"

Ben tried to decipher the meaning behind Jo's shocked expression. His eyes followed hers down to his left leg. A large tooth-shaped shard of glass was buried deep in his thigh like a dagger. He stared down at it and felt his head swim with nausea and confusion. He watched, almost paralyzed, as Jo slowly reached out with both hands and carefully took hold of the piece of glass. She tugged and it came free. Ben watched her drop it on to the Camper van's dashboard and turn to stare back at him.

"You lucky bastard," she said.

She wrapped her knuckles against the hard surface of Ben's prosthetic leg beneath the torn Denim where the glass had gone in. Ben continued to stare at her, gradually letting this sink in.

Jo began to laugh.

"You lucky, lucky bastard."

Ben reached out and squeezed her tightly as she let it all out; her hysterical laughter soon turning to tears. He rocked her gently.

"I'm sorry baby," he whispered.

CHAPTER TWO

Ben stood in front of the Camper van, reaching high into the air with his mobile phone, trying to find a signal, but there was nothing. He lowered his arm and turned to look at Jo, still sitting in the driver's seat with her feet braced against the open door. He shook his head and limped over to her. She was pawing over an unfolded road map as she smoked a cigarette. She had a pair of sunglasses perched on her head, despite the overcast sky above. She looked from the map to the odometer on the dash and back again. Ben took out his tobacco and papers and started rolling.

"It'll probably be dead until we reach Perth," he said.

Ben lit his roll-up and looked at the vast expanse of nothingness surrounding them. He began to feel a pull from its melancholy emptiness, as if he might lose himself altogether in that landscape. The more he looked at the horizon, the less significant everything else seemed. He noticed Jo was up and moving. She folded the map and stuffed it into her daypack with a large bottle of water. She then slipped the pack on to her shoulders and made her way to the rear of the Camper van.

"What are you doing?" said Ben.

Jo started to unpick the cord holding a mountain bike against the carry-frame on the back door.

"Jo?"

She slowly turned to face him, her face tight and braced for trouble, as she lifted the bike off its rack.

"Now, don't lose it with me..." she said. "...But according to the map there's a little coastal town not far away."

"By bike?"

"By bike. Twenty miles if my math is as good as I think it is."

"What?" said Ben. "We're in the middle of nowhere. I haven't even seen any road signs, let alone signs for a town."

"Chill Ben. I checked the map, it's there.

"You can't just cycle off alone out here Jo. What if you got it wrong? What if it's a hundred miles away?"

Jo straddled the bike.

"I'm not wrong," she said. "Look, I reset the odometer at the last fuel stop, I know the mileage."

She watched his expression grow darker.

"Ben."

Ben stepped in front of the bike and rested his hands on the bars.

He sighed.

"OK, I'll go," he said.

Jo smiled at him and looked down at the prosthetic leg hidden in his jeans.

"Yeah, because you love to cycle," she said. "With that, twenty miles really will seem like a hundred.

"Don't do this to me Jo."

"Relax. Deep breaths, like I showed you."

Jo watched her lover try digest this and wrestle down his rising tide of anxiety. She leaned across the handlebars and kissed him, long and slow, and when she pulled back, his breathing was slower, and he was more relaxed.

"I'm going to be fine," she said.

"I'm not happy you know."

"I know," she said, smiling again.

Ben watched helplessly as she cycled around him in a wide arc, before circling back on to the road.

"What's this town called?" he said.

"Sweetwater," said Jo.

"If you don't see any signs in a couple of hours, head back. I don't want you out there in the dark."

"Relax old man."

She struck out on the road, heading in the direction they'd been driving.

"There'll probably be a car along any minute," he called.

Jo waved at him from the bike without looking back.

He watched her slowly diminish to a speck as she rode away, engulfed by the endless landscape.

*

Ben paced around in circles with an agitated limp, smoking relentlessly. He stared out along the road towards the horizon, straining to see Jo, even though he knew she wasn't there.

He watched the sun slowly edge higher through the sky and dropped his last roll-up into the sand with the other butts he'd accumulated. He ground it out with the heel of his trainer and then sat down in the open side of the Camper van. He pulled off his t-shirt, then his trainers and jeans. He sat back down in his boxer shorts and looked at the prosthetic left leg fastened just above where his knee used to be. He detached the device and stared at the naked flesh where his left thigh finished. The gleaming white stump was a sharp contrast to the rest of his tanned skin. His dirty secret, his ever-present reminder of the man he had once been; of the man he despised. He sighed and held the detached prosthetic leg in both hands, bending the knee joint. He hated this instrument almost as much he hated himself. He stared out along the empty road in the direction Jo had left again, but there was still no sign of her.

*

Ben slept. He was dreaming again. His closed eyes danced beneath their lids, as his recurrent nightmare took hold of him again. A flush of sweat covered his forehead, as if he were fighting a fever. A distant noise, a car engine, reached into his troubled subconscious and joined the jumbled narrative there. He moaned and stirred. His wild, scared eyes snapped open to face the world. Ben sat up with a start. He looked down to see he was wearing both his prosthetic leg and his clothes. He hobbled out on to the roadside. In the distance, a battered old recovery truck bounced along the bitumen. Ben squinted at the vehicle as it drew nearer, until he could finally make out Jo riding in the passenger seat. He let out a long-held breath and allowed himself a smile.

The recovery truck swung in way too close to the Camper van and skidded to a halt, forcing Ben backwards. Jo jumped out of the cab and joined him. He mouthed "You're great" at her. Jo smiled back, feigning shyness.

"See," she said, jabbing her finger into his chest. "I told you I'm great."

A gruff, Australian voice interrupted the reconciliation almost immediately.

"You really managed to put her in the ground, eh?"

Ben turned and watched an aging, tall drink of water approach them and slowly circle the Camper van, inspecting the damage. The older man wiped his hands on a dirty rag and stuffed it into the pocket of his greasy blue overalls. He then took a cigarette from behind his ear and lit it. He continued to walk around the vehicle, stopping to bend and tut every now and then.

"Well, Mister..." said Ben.

"Lonesome," said the older man.

"Well, Mr. Lonesome, what do you think?

Lonesome slowly turned his head towards Ben and snorted with contempt, before spitting on the ground.

CHAPTER THREE

Lonesome kept his eyes on the road as they drove on through the empty Nullarbor Plain. Ben rolled himself another cigarette and Jo fidgeted awkwardly, squashed in tightly between the two men. Ben glanced at their Camper van in the rear-view mirror, its impacted front raised and suspended by a large winch. He was no mechanic, but it looked bad. A distorted aria crackled from Lonesome's thin, tinny radio speakers, making the sound almost unbearable. Ben placed his cigarette in his mouth and prepared to light it, when he noticed Lonesome staring at him.

"There's no smoking in my truck," said the mechanic.

"Sorry," said Ben. "I thought you were a smoker."

"I am," he said.

"So," said Jo. "How long will it take to fix Lonesome?"

"I reckon you'll be bunking in town for a couple of days at least," said the mechanic. "I won't know the worst of it until I get her into the workshop."

Ben and Jo glanced at each other but said nothing. They then both fixed their eyes on the road ahead.

Lonesome's truck peeled off the main bitumen road under heavy grey skies and took a gravel track that forked off and gradually wound its way out towards the coast. Ben saw a rickety hand-painted sign at the edge of the track:

Sweetwater - 33 km.

The music on Lonesome's radio began to break down into a series of long crackles, before finally dissolving altogether into a rising and falling wave of whining static as the signal ebbed. Lonesome finally turned the volume down, but the faint and eerie sound was still there, lingering in the background.

"Ain't nothing works out here," said Lonesome. "Not anymore."

*

Ben stared out through the truck's window as they passed a rundown trailer park just off the coastal road. It looked more like a graveyard for caravans, than a working holiday site. Beyond the park, jagged cliff edges stretched out towards the sea, trying, but failing to obscure the bleak and tumultuous Bight.

Lonesome looked at the trailer park and revealed a callous grin.

"Irma's place, he said. "Cheap enough, if you can stand all the chit-chat."

Lonesome's truck reached his dilapidated petrol station and garage just as dusk began to devour day. They passed the petrol pumps and pulled up in front of a large junkyard and workshop. Semi-cannibalized vehicles and rusting, discarded parts littered the area. Lonesome eased himself out of the cab and released the clamps on the back of the truck.

"She'll be at least a few days," he said. "There's a hotel on the other side of town, or you can use Irma's, depending on your budget."

Ben and Jo looked at each other, and then at the few twinkling lights of Sweetwater's main street in the distance.

"Any chance of a lift?" said Ben.

"Nah," said Lonesome. "I've got to get this squared away and then close up."

Lonesome took the Camper van out of park and thumbed a large remote to operate the winch suspending it. The Camper van slowly rolled off the back of the truck as it lowered. Ben and Jo reluctantly grabbed their backpacks from the truck's cab and circled around to watch their Camper van being unhooked.

Lonesome eyed Ben's limp.

"If you banged your leg, we've got a doctor in town."

Ben tapped on the false leg with his knuckles. Lonesome looked down at the ground and then magically pulled another cigarette from behind his ear. He wet it with his lips.

"Surfer, eh?" he said. "That's a bad business. We get a lot of that around here."

Without another word, Lonesome pulled up the workshop's metal shutter and disappeared inside.

Ben and Jo exchanged looks of disbelief and then began walking towards town.

*

Ben and Jo emerged from the darkness as they approached the edge of Sweetwater's main street. The rundown thoroughfare was reminiscent of ghost towns in old western movies. Many of the streetlamps were out, leaving only a few scant pools of light defying the night. Most of the dilapidated, wooden properties inhabiting the street were boarded up, seemingly abandoned. Ben eyed a tired looking store that still had a glass frontage:

Olanders

There was no sign of life within though, and a thick coating of dust covered the shop's windows. Ben and Jo trudged on with their packs through the shadows.

A few moments later they reached a bar, or rather a menacing looking lit doorway wedged between two abandoned buildings. There was a circular sign above the door with the words:

The Black Cat

There was a silhouette of a black cat leaping across a white background; chasing something, or being chased. The wind began to pick up. It lifted a fine cloud of dust into the night air, blowing it across the high street.

They both eyed the creaking sign with suspicion.

"C'mon," whispered Jo. "I'm not *that* thirsty."

Ben and Jo left the glare of the last working streetlight and found themselves swallowed by the darkness again.

They passed through to the other side of town and made their way up a winding, decaying road that hugged the cliff edges, as it rose up over the town. They paused and looked back down at the remaining lights of Sweetwater. They could hear the waves of the Bight crashing against the foot of the cliffs far below. They gazed out at a fat, silvery moon reflected on the dark, open waters that surrounded the town. They then turned and continued up towards the outline of a large, lone house that sat on the highest cliff edge, overlooking both the town and the sea that bordered it. Jo and Ben stared up at the opulent, but faded Victorian hotel. Jo snuggled into Ben against the high winds that toyed with the hotel's sign.

It read:

Ho's Palace

"Classy," said Jo.

A light flicked on behind the raised porch and a large figure appeared in the closed doorway there. The silhouette inside looked misshapen through the dimpled glass that revealed it. The door opened and a tall, very sturdy looking woman stepped out on to the porch to greet them. The late middle-aged woman looked more like a builder in drag in a plain and shapeless dress that hung from her square shoulders. The woman spoke in a thick, Australian accent.

"How's it going?" she said.

"Good, thanks," said Jo. "Have you got any rooms free?"

"Only all of 'em. Come on in. I'm Angie."

"Jo and Ben."

Angie Ho easily lifted both backpacks off the pair and about turned to carry them inside. Ben and Jo followed her into Ho's Palace, both surprised by the woman's strength.

"This is a nice surprise, we don't normally get visitors this time of year," said Angie. "C'mon, it's turning nasty out there."

Angie Ho pushed through the front door and into a large, garishly decorated reception hall. The house may have been Victorian, but the furnishings inside were pure seventies. The walls hummed with fiercely patterned wallpaper and chintzy furniture seemed to be crammed into every available space. Ben instinctively lingered by a studded, leather fronted reception counter and tried to look at the entries in the open guest book on top.

"Hello there, welcome."

Ben and Jo turned to face a small white-haired Polynesian man advancing on them from the other end of the hall. The aging hotelier quickly offered them his hand, the glare of his wide, white grin competing with his equally bright Hawaiian shirt. He shook hands with Jo, then with Ben, and his smile grew even wider.

"It's so nice to meet you," he said. "My name is Henry Ho and this, is Ho's Palace."

Ben gritted his teeth to keep any sarcastic remarks at bay.

"Hi Henry, I'm Jo Bridgewater and this is Ben Barker."

"You're together?" said Ho.

"Err...yes, yes we're together."

"Ahhh excellent. One less bed to make, eh?

Jo nodded with embarrassment, but found herself smiling with bewilderment at the same time. Ben watched Ho carefully. The grinning little man didn't seem quite so funny anymore. Angie Ho let out an exaggerated sigh from halfway up the staircase.

"Let go of 'em Henry," she said. "They just got here for Christ sakes."

Ho shot his wife a quick, icy look, and then the stick-on-grin was back with a vengeance. He turned back to face his guests again.

"Please, would you join my wife and I for dinner tonight? No extra charge, of course."

Ben and Jo were caught out. They stared at each other for a moment, trying to read each other's thoughts.

"Thanks Mr. Ho," said Jo eventually. "That would be lovely."

"Excellent," said Ho. "We'll see you down here in an hour."

Ho watched them carefully as they ascended the stairs, maintaining his grin until they were out of sight. Then he let it slide from his face, as his shoulders slumped with resignation. He trudged back the way he came towards the end of the hall, methodically filling a pipe with tobacco as he went.

Angie Ho barged up two more steep flights of stairs with the full packs, and then along another chintzy hallway landing, all without missing a breath. Ben and Jo followed her past a half a dozen closed doors.

"You two married?" asked Angie.

"No," said Jo, frowning with confusion.

"Shame. I was going to put you in the honeymoon suite. Ah what the heck, I'll tell Henry you're practicing."

The large woman winked at Jo and kicked open the door to the honeymoon suite. She dumped the packs on a pink, heart shaped bed that appeared to have been around since the sixties. Ben and Jo stood in the doorway and took a moment to drink in the cupid peppered red wallpaper, lace doilies and half-melted, scented candles. Angie Ho marched over to the window and drew back a floor to ceiling set of velvet curtains. She opened up the windows behind them to let in the sound of huge waves pounding into the rocks below.

"Better let it air out for a bit, it's been a while," she said, then pointed to another doorway.

"Bathroom's through there. So, I guess we'll see you downstairs in a bit, OK?"

Jo smiled and nodded and received two door keys for her trouble. Then Angie Ho was out of the room and away, hauling her heavy carcass down the stairs with great, thumping footsteps. Ben and Jo flopped down on to the heart-shaped bed and searched each other's straight faces for any hint of humor. Jo cracked first, and then Ben joined in, as they both collapsed into fits of hysterical giggles.

CHAPTER FOUR

Jo and Ben sat with Henry Ho in a chintzy lounge that was idiosyncratic to say the least. The walls were adorned with framed maps and aerial photographs of the Hawaiian Islands, tall potted palms sprouted from the corners of the room like set dressing from a nineteen twenties drawing room, and the carpet's mind-altering puzzle pattern reminded Ben of the Overlook Hotel in The Shining. Ho rose and moved to a large mahogany atlas globe stationed by the wall. He slid back most of the western hemisphere to reveal an array of half-finished spirit bottles.

"What'll it be?" he said. The hospitality grin was still out, but on low beam now.

"Beer, please," said Jo.

"Whiskey's good," said Ben.

Jo shot Ben a concerned look. He caught it and returned something more condescending than reassuring. Ho turned around and handed them their drinks, before settling back into the armchair opposite with a glass of beer.

"Cheers," he said.

"Cheers."

"So," said Ho. "You had yourselves a little car trouble, eh?"

"Yeah," said Jo, slightly taken back. "Erm...?"

"It's a small town, word gets around fast," said Ho. "Besides, no one would deliberately come here now. The town's dead enough in season."

"Our Camper van's with Lonesome, in town," said Jo.

"Mmmm," said Ho. "He's not much of a talker, but he's a decent mechanic. Me, I like to talk. I love meeting people. That's why I went into the hotel business."

"So, things are slow?" said Ben.

"Everywhere along the Bight's slow. This is a tough time of year; we just batten down the hatches and sit tight."

"I noticed a lot of vacant places in town," said Ben.

"Yeah," said Ho. "Well, Sweetwater's had a pretty bad run of luck. Actually, that's wrong, it was always unlucky. Things have just been particularly bad over the last few years."

"How so?" said Jo.

Ho returned to the globe-bar and refilled his glass from a stash of beer cans in a fridge disguised as a mahogany cupboard beneath.

"Refill?"

His smile was gone now.

Ben drained his whiskey glass and nodded.

"When the weather's good, this is a beautiful place to be. The people are warm and the views out here, they're fantastic. It's like you're standing on the edge of the world. You like surfing? Now, I don't indulge myself, but I *am* from Hawaii."

Ho handed Ben a very generous double and leaned in to wink at him.

"Let me tell you," he whispered. "Sweetwater has great surfing. The best."

"Well, that must bring in a lot of tourist dollars?" said Ben.

"No," said Ho. "Not really. The Bight's a cruel place. Nature's cruel. And you don't get something for nothing."

Ho raised both hands to gesture, keeping a firm hold of his beer.

"You see, we have pointers to the east, and tigers to the west. And in the middle, Sweetwater's got the worst of both."

"What's a pointer?" said Jo.

"Sharks," said Ben. "He's talking about sharks."

"There's always been trouble in these waters. You ask anyone along the coast. But people still have to live their lives, take acceptable risks."

"But...?" said Ben.

"Like I said, a couple of years ago, we had too much trouble all at once. The press got a hold of it and milked it good. When they were done, we were officially a black spot, a pariah. Of course, the drama blew over eventually, but the memories always linger. Nowadays, most people don't know we're here, but those that do know tend to steer well clear of the town. A few of us have stayed on to make a go of it, but...you know."

Ho shrugged his shoulders and sipped his beer.

"I think I'll give the sea a miss tomorrow," said Jo. "No offence."

Ho bowed his head slightly to her.

"None taken."

Sensing a presence, Ben looked up to see Angie Ho's frame filling the doorway. She held a large plastic spatula in her hand; its end was melted and misshapen.

"Thanks for the drink, Love," she said, sarcastically.

Ho leapt up and was at the bar in seconds, fixing his wife a drink.

"Sorry Ange," he said.

"Is he putting the frighteners on you?" said Angie. "There's nothing wrong with the waters around here. I've been swimming off this coast all my life and I've never had any trouble."

Ho handed his wife a beer.

"Be fair Love," he said. "There's not many sharks that would want to tangle with you."

The big woman laughed.

"Yeah. Talk about biting off more than you can chew."

Ben and Jo watched the Ho's laugh and took this as a signal it was OK to join in.

Ben, Jo, and Henry and Angie Ho moved to an equally garish dining room, where they all sat around a large table eating platefuls of fried fish. The two couples chatted through a mercifully short evening, dominated by alcohol and Henry Ho's anecdotes, as the hotelier's hosting skills went into overdrive. All the time an enormous, sprawling, fake crystal chandelier hung over their heads, like some monstrous jellyfish suspended in mid-attack.

*

Ben and Jo lay awake in their heart-shaped bed by candlelight, listening to the boom of waves pounding the rocks and caves below.

"That was a pretty decent finish to a shitty day," said Jo.

"So, am I forgiven for earlier?" said Ben.

She kissed his forehead.

"You're a sarcastic bastard, so I guess you can't help it. Am I forgiven for crashing the van and stranding us in Eerie Indiana?"

Ben looked pensive, as his thoughts trailed off into the past. Jo screwed her face up in a wince, and then nodded to herself.

"Sorry. That was pretty insensitive, wasn't it?"

"No. No it's fine."

"You sure?"

Ben nodded.

Jo slid her hands under the covers.

"Hey," she said. "You know this *is* the honeymoon suite."

"Yeah?"

"Oh yeah," she said, kissing him on the mouth.

"And apparently, we can only stay here, if we *practice*."

They kissed again, deeper this time.

Neither of them noticed the tiniest trickle of light escaping from the wall opposite. And neither of them saw the unblinking eye staring at them from the peephole there, hidden amongst the jazzy pattern of red hearts and floating cupids.

CHAPTER FIVE

The next day in Sweetwater the skies were clear, but still grey. Jo stood alone near the edge of the cliffs, staring at the ocean. Below her, a two-hundred-foot sheer drop led to jagged, teeth-like rocks where the water crashed and churned. Ben emerged from Ho's Palace and lingered on the porch, watching her stare out to sea. He pulled his daypack over his shoulder and limped towards her. He felt good. Yesterday had been a bad day; the crash, being stranded, his relationship-sabotaging sarcasm, but they'd come through it in one piece. Sure, they were stuck in this weird little town, but maybe a few days break from being on the road would be a good thing for both of them. For his part, he could work on his defense mechanisms and take the time to remind Jo why he was worth sticking with. He came up behind her quietly and slipped an arm around her waist.

"Careful," he said.

Jo looked at him and smiled. They instinctively folded into each other in an embrace. Yes, a good day. They turned away together and made their way back down the winding coastal road towards town.

Lonesome's workshop was shut up when they arrived. A large piece of card was wedged into the metal shutter that had been rolled only halfway down.

"Back soon" was scrawled on the card in faded marker pen ink. As an afterthought, "ish" had been added to the end of the statement.

Jo looked forlornly at the sign, and then at their Camper van parked outside. It had been stripped down to the bare bodywork and frame, and its components lay scattered across the ground around it. Ben emerged from the dim interior of Lonesome's garage and shrugged at her. He stood next to her and stared at the mechanical remains of their vehicle.

"We need to find him," he said.

"We could try town," said Jo.

Ben nodded and quietly clenched his fist, trying not to show Jo his rising anger.

*

Main Street turned out to be nearly as empty as Lonesome's workshop, as Ben and Jo strolled into town. There was just one person in sight: a tiny old woman clutching a beaded shopping bag with both hands. The old woman motored past them with speedy little micro-steps like some wind-up geisha, pausing only briefly to nod her head at them in the briefest of acknowledgments.

"Where the hell is he?" said Ben.

"Maybe he went to the beach," said Jo.

"Yeah, right," said Ben.

Ben felt the sharp sarcasm on his tongue before he knew it was there.

"OK," he said, trying to rescue himself. "Let's give it try."

But his face was now as overcast as the sky above them, and he knew Jo could see one of his moods brewing.

Damn van, he thought.

They walked down to a deserted stretch of unkempt beach and stood there looking out to sea. A lone surfer was out amongst the waves tackling eight-foot peaks with aplomb. Ben and Jo looked at each other. They both remembered their talk with Ho the night before and shared a grimace, wondering what else might be lurking in the water with the surfer.

They walked on along the beach. Jo slipped her sandals off and began to flirt with the tide at the water's edge. She feigned a little pantomime hysteria when the cold water caught her toes, trying to distract Ben from his souring mood and make him lighten up. He didn't want to play though, choosing instead to lag behind, picking his way through the sand, lost in introspection. Thoughts of yesterday's crash circled is mind. It was an accident, or if anyone was to blame, it was surely that idiot driving the white van on their side of the road. So why was he suddenly so angry with Jo? She'd just done what anyone else would have done. Her quick reactions had actually prevented them from being injured. So why the hell did he feel this way towards her? Something caught his eye and he stopped to stare out at the waves. For a moment, he was sure he could see a large shadow rising through the water behind the surfer.

Then it was gone.

He quickly scanned the water again, but could see nothing. Jo appeared behind him and traced his gaze.

"What is it?" she said. "Oh my God."

"What?" said Ben.

This time Ben followed her eye line, out to the blond-haired surfer riding the wave in. One of the man's two legs planted firmly on the surfboard was a prosthetic. It was a customized sports model. The wiry, black plastic leg bent in time with the flesh driving it, as the surfer shifted his weight and controlled his balance of the board.

"That's amazing," said Jo.

"Yes," said Ben, quietly. "Yes, it is."

Ben rolled himself a cigarette while they waited for the surfer to make his way in. The surfer waved a lithe, muscular arm at them, as he waded from the water. Jo waved back. The surfer made his way up the beach and planted his board in the sand. He smiled and reached out to shake Jo's hand, then Ben's.

"Leyton," he said. "How's it going?"

"Hi," said Jo, gushing more than a little. "I'm Jo, this is Ben. And that, that was very, very cool."

"Ah, you know," said Leyton. "It shakes the morning cobwebs loose."

Leyton motioned further down the beach.

"Do you guys fancy a coffee? Crazy should be up by now."

Jo looked at Ben, who just sighed smoke into the air.

"Sure," she said. "Thanks."

"Cool," said Leyton. "I love meeting tourists, it's a rare chance to catch up on reality. We're pretty cut off out here."

Leyton and Jo smiled at his well-worn icebreaker, while Ben just stared into the sand. The three of them then started along the empty beach, Ben lagging behind. As they walked, Ben noticed a large wooden shack up ahead. It was set back against the road, where the sand rose and undulated in great sloping dunes. A big, bold, but tired sign in faded gold paint declared:

Crazy's Golf

Sure enough, behind the shack, Ben could just make out something that might have passed for a crazy golf course; although it could also pass for a scrap yard with golf flags. Ben eyed Leyton's limp. It wasn't exactly the same as his, but it was close, and the two men kept in step as they walked. Leyton caught him staring, but the Aussie said nothing, he just grinned.

"I hope you don't mind me asking," said Jo. "But aren't these waters dangerous for surfing?"

"Well, they're dangerous for anything," said Leyton.

"So why go out there?"

Leyton shrugged.

"I love to surf," he said. "And you can't live your life properly if you're scared all the time, can you?"

Ben exhaled another plume of smoke and kept his surly gaze fixed on the wooden shack ahead.

"Besides," said Leyton, looking down at his false leg. "They've already had a taste of me, and they didn't like it. Me Ma says I'm stringy."

Ben, Jo and Leyton stood outside Crazy's tumbledown beach shack-cum-office-cum-coffee counter. The shutters were up, and the stools were out on the beach-side of the counter, but the interior of the shack was dark and lifeless. Ben looked at the golf course behind the shack. It was a variation on crazy golf, remade from junk and flotsam; scrap and corrugated metal, driftwood, recycled plastic, oil drums and a mishmash of wood off-cuts had been roughly assembled to form nine whole holes of golf.

Leyton banged on the counter and shouted.

"Crazy, ya drunken bum. Get up."

Leyton hopped on to the nearest stool and delved into a plastic box of sauces and cutlery. He fished out a faded sachet of sugar, ripping it open and sprinkling it on his tongue. Ben and Jo sat on the adjacent stools, as a low, menacing groan rose from the interior of the shack, interrupted halfway through by a wet belch. A figure shuffled out of the dark, growling with an American accent.

"You're too early kid,"

"It's not early man," said Leyton. "It's late. Anyway, I've brought you some customers."

"Oh yeah?"

A haggard, aging Lothario emerged from the shadows. His tired brown eyes were set in a face like tanned leather, creased by the lines of a life lived a little too well. Crazy had two- or three-days grey growth and if he was past sixty, his tailor hadn't got the memo; last night's stained and flared polyester suit, his flamboyant gold rings and a medallion nestled amongst a mat of grey chest hair hinted that there was still life in the old dog yet.

"Tearing one off again last night, eh old man?"

Crazy burped again and fiddled with his crotch.

"Who's this?" he said.

"Jo and Ben," said Jo. "Nice to meet you Crazy."

"Delighted," said the old man. "I was called Joe once."

Crazy looked over Ben's scars, then without a word, he filled the kettle under the tap, flicked it on and unscrewed the top from an unseen bottle behind the counter. He poured quickly and Ben caught the flash of a whiskey magically disappearing in a heartbeat. Crazy sighed and wiped his mouth with the back of his hand. He caught Ben watching him, but neither man said anything. Leyton pulled a cheap, canvas sports bag from behind the counter and began rummaging in it. Crazy poured himself another rescue whiskey and noticed Ben was still watching him.

"Something to say?" he said.

Ben feigned disinterest and looked away down the beach. Leyton retrieved a joint from his bag and lit it, blowing smoke towards Crazy.

"I see you're in a good mood again," he said.

"You know where the coffee is," said the old man. "I need another hour.

Crazy turned around and shuffled back into the shadows, as Leyton stifled a giggle and passed the joint to Jo. Ben lit another cigarette and sighed smoke into the air with a disapproving sigh. Jo gave him a cold look in return. She held his gaze and then took a long drag on the joint.

*

Ben stared at the sea from his spot in the sand, watching large waves tumble and crash on the shoreline. The roar of the surf filled his ears, but he could still hear Jo and Leyton giggling as they got high. They lay on their fronts in the sand a few feet ahead of him, cracking up over something apparently hilarious.

"Hey," said Leyton. "I think you're burning."

Leyton squirted a glob of cold sun lotion over Jo's back making her squeal. He began to slowly massage it into her skin. Jo suddenly looked embarrassed.

"Erm..."

"You know," he said. "Just because it's overcast, it doesn't mean you're safe, your skin will still burn."

Ben slowly rose from the sand and approached them.

"That's enough," he said.

Leyton ignored him for a moment, before pushing himself up and brushing away the sand from his body. He stepped forwards, going toe to toe with Ben, the two men locked in a stare.

Leyton grinned at him.

"You want to relax mate," said Leyton. "You'll live longer."

Jo stood up and put herself between the two men. Leyton maintained his stare for a few moments to drive the point home, then turned to her.

"I think I'll take a dip. Catch you later Jo."

Ben watched the surfer limp out across the sand and into the ocean. He could feel Jo's eyes burning into him. He reluctantly turned to face her, and the music.

"Don't look at me like that," he said. "He was hitting on you."

"Yeah, he was hitting on *me*, and *I* was in control of it. I don't need you charging in on your white horse, trying to fight every man I talk to."

"He had his hands all over you, right in front of me."

Jo took a deep breath and looked away for a moment, trying her best to remain calm.

"We agreed you were going to make an effort Ben, let me handle my own life."

"But he was trying..."

"No more protecting, no more controlling."

She looked him in the eye.

"No more jealousy."

"But his hands..."

"For Christ's sake," she said. "He was just putting sun cream on my back."

Jo sighed with frustration.

"Just stop Ben. OK? Just stop."

She looked at his dark, manic eyes. They were filled with so much guilt and fear.

"Don't you trust me?" she said.

Ben lowered his gaze and stared at the sand. Jo drew closer and took his jaw in her hand. She raised it, forcing eye contact. She looked into Ben's eyes again. This time she saw doubt swimming behind them. Jo quickly turned away and snatched up her shoes. She marched away down the beach without another word.

"Jo," called Ben. "Jo, wait."

That was a big mistake he thought. Sure, you made your point, but at what cost? Panic flared and burned through his chest as he realized he'd really done it this time. He grabbed the daypack and limped after her, calling out again, but Jo quickened her pace in response and soon outstripped him. Ben lagged further and further behind as she walked away from him down the beach. He eventually halted, cursing under his breath.

He turned around and reluctantly headed up a small track leading back towards town. As he left the beach, he didn't notice the small, grey thing carried up on to the shore with the tide, riding the surf in. The sea withdrew seconds later, leaving a woman's severed foot washed up on the wet sand. As the water retreated it wobbled and flopped over on to its side.

*

Jo kept walking, trying to cool off. She wandered further up the beach and then circled around the foot of the cliffs at the headland to find the next stretch of coastline. A rough shingle beach lay on the other side. It led up to another rocky outcrop that jutted out into the sea. She made her way along this second shingle beach and climbed over the rocks there. Beyond them she could see an old, dilapidated boathouse, then what looked like a cannery with a rotting pier in the distance.

She took a deep breath and reeled as the thick stench of rotting fish hit her. She then heard a buzzing chorus and hundreds of flies lifted into the air around her. Jo quickly stumbled away over the rocks and tried to cut inland, away from the flies. She followed a track there back up to a gravel road and saw that it gradually wound down towards town and away from the cliffs.

Jo reached the top of the track and climbed up on to the road. She stood there sizing up both directions it had to offer. To the east, she could see Ho's Palace and the cliffs she had already navigated. Beyond that was Sweetwater. To the west, there lay an even more desolate stretch of coastline, where the rundown cannery and what was left of the pier lay.

She started the long walk back to the hotel, when she noticed another figure also heading towards it in the distance. She recognized Ben's tell-tale limp straight away; and he was the last person she wanted to see.

"You shit, Ben," she said to herself, as she turned around and walked away in the opposite direction.

CHAPTER SIX

Ben made his way back up to Ho's Palace under a dark, threatening sky. When he reached the front door, he found it unlocked and caught by the rising wind, banging back and forth in its frame. Ben entered the gloomy reception and forced it shut behind him, squeezing out the whistling, protesting gusts. The hall light snapped on to reveal Mr. Ho staring sternly at him over the top of his reading glasses. Ben noticed a tumbler of whiskey in Ho's hand and the man's glassy eyes, and quickly realised he was drunk.

"It's getting pretty nasty out there again," said Ben.

"Welcome to our world," said Ho. He rattled the ice in his empty glass. "Tempt you to a drink?"

"Thanks, but it's a bit early."

"Just a quick one."

Ho moved closer and gave him a conspiratorial wink.

"It'd be just as well to let her cool off for a bit."

"Sorry?"

"I know that expression," said Ho. "You've got woman troubles. Come on."

Ben looked up the empty staircase, and then back at Ho, wondering if Jo had already returned to the hotel ahead of him, perhaps cursing or crying, or maybe both. He felt his face redden with embarrassment and nodded to Ho. He followed the older man back to the lounge behind the reception area, where Ho poured out two very generous measures of whiskey. Ben moved to sit on the couch, but Ho shook his head and motioned for him to follow again. Ho picked up the bottle and they walked through a large, clean, but dated yellow and white kitchen, and then along another chintzy passageway, half-lit by a row of small, ornate wall lamps.

"Every man should have a den," said Ho. "Especially when he's in the doghouse."

Ho pushed open a door at the end of the passage to reveal a roomy old study. This dark, serious chamber was a sharp contrast to the rest of the hotel, with rows and rows of mahogany shelving crammed with aging books, and paintings and framed photos hung on the walls. Hawaiian artifacts and stacks of files cluttered every surface, even the floor, giving the impression of either compulsive hoarding, or a major scholarly work in progress. Ho navigated around a desk and several tall stacks of floor-bound paperwork to find a high-backed leather chair. Ben followed him and took a second, less impressive chair across the desk from him.

"You a writer?" asked Ben.

"A scholar," said Ho.

Ben made sure he nodded, even if he didn't quite understand what that meant in Ho's case.

"You and Jo," said Ho. "Is it the real thing?"

"Come again."

"Is she the one?"

Ben hesitated for a minute, taken back by the question.

"Angie and I might look like a strange match," said Ho. "But I knew it was going to be her from the first time we ever met. There was never a doubt in my mind."

"That's good," said Ben.

"It's more than just good," said Ho. "It's the way it's got to be."

The two men drank their whiskies and Ben's eyes broke away and roamed across the spines of the various volumes filling the shelves. They then lifted and settled on a magnificent, ornately framed painting on the wall and grew wide with awe. It was a romantic depiction of a muscular Hawaiian brave wrestling in water against a thrashing tiger shark almost double his size. Man and shark appeared to be pitted against each other in a darkened underground cave that had been carved out and flooded to form a sunken, gladiatorial arena.

A low rumble of thunder grumbled from the skies above them, making Ben tense up.

"Jesus," he said.

"You like it?" said Ho.

"Like's maybe the wrong word. What is it?"

"Ancient tradition. Where I come from man always strived for harmony with the sea. If that harmony was lost, man would have to appease the king of the sea, show him there should be mutual respect."

"A sacrifice?"

"Not exactly."

Ho rose and walked over to one of the bookcases. He stretched up and pulled a glass case down from the top shelf, then returned, holding it up for Ben to see. Inside was a large single shark's tooth, mounted on the end of a short wooden handle to form some sort of ancient weapon.

Ben stared at it in disbelief.

"You might say it was similar to a bull fight," said Ho. "Except the gladiator had only one hope. To hold his nerve until the final moment of the tiger's charge. He would then have to dive beneath the great fish and gut it in that single pass. Otherwise he would almost certainly be ripped to pieces."

Ho put the glass case down on the desk between them and sat back down. Ben stared at it, and then up at the painting again. The warrior there wielded a similar token weapon against the shark's gaping jaws of dagger-like teeth. There was another rumble of thunder overhead.

"I can't imagine they had many volunteers," said Ben.

"They were different times," said Ho. "Men went to extraordinary lengths to feed and protect their loved ones every day."

Ho downed his whiskey. He sighed and poured himself another large one.

"You OK?" said Ben.

Ho seemed to be dazed, introspective, as if he'd forgotten Ben's presence for a moment. Ho slowly looked up at him with a sad, almost lost expression. An oppressive silence descended over the room, and it was while before either of them spoke again.

"I don't suppose you want to buy a hotel, do you?" said Ho, eventually. "I'll give you a good price."

Ho began to chuckle to himself, so much that he started to tremble. Ben watched, feeling more and more uncomfortable, sure that the other man was about to burst into tears.

"I should go," he said. "Thanks for the drink."

Ben stood up and limped out, unable to look Ho in the eye. He left the hotel and wandered out to the cliff edge. There, he stood and smoked and watched the black storm clouds gathering over the sea, as he wondered what he could say to appease Jo.

*

It was dark when Ben finally returned to their room. He slowly opened the door and peeked inside, wary of the reception he might get. Jo was already in bed, but she was fully dressed and reading by lamp light. Their gear lay in the centre of the room, packed and ready to go. He stared at it and felt dread thicken in the pit of his stomach. He approached Jo, his mind racing to find the right words he'd need to make her stay.

"Look," he said. "I'm sorry about earlier."

Jo glared at him.

"I...I was..."

Jo's eyes widened and she slowly raised her index finger to her lips. Ben's brow creased in confusion. She held his stare and silently rose from the bed, then crept over to the wall opposite. She motioned for him to join her and then pointed to an area of it at roughly head height. Ben leant in and examined the busily patterned wallpaper. There, set amongst the flying cupids and hearts, was a peephole drilled into the wall. The couple stared at it and then at each other for a long time, as the meaning of this slowly sank in.

*

Angie Ho stood out on the porch, silhouetted by the light spilling from the hotel reception behind her. She watched Ben and Jo shoulder their packs and head out into the night and the driving rain. Thunder rumbled somewhere above them in the blackness.

"Are you sure you don't want to stay tonight?" she called. "You're all paid up."

Ben raised his hand without looking back and waved away the idea. Henry Ho watched them leave with cold fascination from an upstairs window. His hard stare tracked them as they slogged towards town through the torrential downpour.

Ben and Jo were both soaked to the skin within seconds of leaving the hotel. They didn't hurry, resigning themselves to the weather, but in silent agreement that it was a small price to pay to be out of the suddenly creepy hotel. They trudged down Sweetwater's high street, as the driving rain sparkled beneath the few remaining patches of lamp light. The only sign of life around was distorted jazz music blaring out of the doorway of The Black Cat saloon.

"I can't believe I felt sorry for that dirty old bastard," said Ben. "Do you think he was watching us last night?"

Jo kept walking. She didn't even look in Ben's direction.

"You're still not talking to me then?" he said.

Jo remained silent, focused solely on the way ahead.

"I'll take that as a no then."

CHAPTER SEVEN

The drenched couple walked through to the other side of town and carried on, heading further and further away from the few lights visible on Sweetwater's dark landscape. Heavy rain hammered the road's surface and pelted the surrounding dirt, as more thunder broke across the sky and out to sea, competing against the crash of waves bursting over the rocks lining the coast. A white van crawled slowly behind Ben and Jo, keeping its distance, its headlights off. In the darkness and the deluge, neither of them saw the freezer van that had run them off the road the day before.

Eventually the rainfall slowed. It finally stopped as Ben and Jo reached an arched gate, bearing the sign:

Irma's Caravan Park

Ben looked up into the black sky above, as the last few drops of rain spat and ceased, as if to say, *really, now?* They walked through the gate and made their way past rows of dirty, abandoned looking caravans, and towards the more welcoming light of the park office. Ben pushed the office door and heard its hinges squeal all the way open. He stepped into a drab, but tidy little reception followed by Jo. The walls there were plastered with an abundance of typed notices, lists, rules and reminders, but the paper bearing them looked brittle and yellow with age. Jo stepped in front of Ben without looking at him and slapped the desk bell, releasing a dull ping. Footsteps shuffled up to a closed door behind the office counter and it opened to reveal a late middle-aged woman wearing a pastel pink jogging suit with a matching headband. When the woman stepped into the light, Ben was taken aback by the quantity of badly applied make-up caked on her face. It should have been funny, but it was just disturbing. There was a name badge pinned to her jogging suit.

It read: Irma.

"Hi Irma," said Ben.

Irma smiled at them and pointed to a tariff, clumsily chalked in a childlike scrawl on a blackboard set against the wall. Jo managed to smile back, then studied the price list. Irma slowly ran her finger down against the options on the blackboard. Jo nodded when the older woman's finger pointed to "On-site vans" and Irma nodded to confirm. Jo let her wet pack slide down to the floor and retrieved a small roll of cash from the top pocket. Irma pulled open her jogging top to reveal a note pad and pen hanging on a bootlace around her neck. She tore off a sheet and began writing on it. When she was finished, she put it on the counter for Jo to read. As Jo looked, Irma gave Ben a coy, sideways glance, as if she were a shy teenager.

The note read "$60 a night. How long?"

"We'll just take tonight for now and let you know tomorrow," said Jo. "OK?"

Irma nodded enthusiastically and took the money from Jo with a sickly grin. She then grabbed a stack of sheets and blankets from behind the counter and made for the door. Ben tried to make eye contact with Jo, but she just looked straight through him and quickly set off outside after Irma.

Irma picked her way through the maze of rotting caravans with precision, as Ben and Jo tried to keep up. Mist rose from the damp ground and clung to their heels after the rain. The sound of crickets filled the trailer park. Irma stopped at one of the cleaner caravans and unlocked it. She reached inside and flicked on a light, then handed the key to Jo.

"Thanks," said Jo.

Ben and Jo stood by the door waiting for Irma to leave, but the strange woman lingered. She stared at them with wide-eyed enthusiasm and an insane grin on her face, looking like some demented clown. Finally, Ben nodded goodnight to her and limped inside the caravan to escape. Jo hesitated and smiled awkwardly at the woman, then did likewise. When she closed the caravan door, Irma's crazed, painted face continued to smile at them from the dark.

Ben kept his distance from Jo, as she drew the curtains and hurriedly stripped off her wet clothes, whipping a towel out of her pack. Her movements were sharp and aggressive. She proceeded to roughly towel her hair dry without looking at him.

"This is stupid," said Ben. "We need to talk about this."

Jo ignored him. She made the bed up with the fresh sheets Irma had supplied, took her creased paperback from her pack and climbed in between the covers. She lay there with her back to him, reading, or at least pretending to. Ben hovered, thinking about approaching her, but deciding against it. His frustration was getting the better of him though, threatening to boil over into anger.

"I said I was sorry," said Ben finally. "Anyway, you were getting high together. He was flirting with you, and you know God damned well you were flirting with him."

Jo kept on reading in silence.

"OK," he said. "Just remember one thing Jo. If I've ever had doubts about you and me, it's because you created them. That's on you."

Ben leant his pack against the wall and left the caravan, slamming the door on the way out, making the whole edifice shake. Outside, He took a deep breath and slowly let it out. He then quickly rolled himself a cigarette. His match flared against the night as he lit it and inhaled. Then he heard it.

Faint music coming from somewhere in the trailer park. He cocked his head to one side and listened intently, trying to pinpoint its source. He scanned the darkness for a moment, and then walked off in what he hoped was the direction it was coming from.

As Ben drew closer, he recognised the music. It was Scott Walker crooning "Best of Both Worlds". He saw a campfire burning up ahead, with two characters silhouetted against it. Crazy and Leyton sat drinking out in front of Crazy's own drab caravan. Both men looked up as Ben approached. Crazy's eyes followed each of Ben's limped steps without reaction. Ben could now see that Leyton was clearly stoned. The surfer just grinned at him with a glassy expression, seemingly unconcerned by their run-in that morning.

"Evening gents," said Ben.

He nodded a greeting to the two men, and they did likewise. Ben warmed himself by the fire and watched the vinyl rotate on a chunky, dated turntable.

"Hey sit down, man," said Leyton. "You're blocking my sun."

Ben sat down on a creaking deckchair next to them. Crazy poured a mug of the hard stuff and passed it to him, without speaking.

"Hey you're pretty wet, mate," said Leyton. "You been for a dip or something?"

"Just been enjoying the weather around here," said Ben.

Leyton leaned forwards and slapped his hand on to Ben's prosthetic knee joint.

"Well better make sure your working parts don't rust."

Crazy shot the stoner a "shut up" look, but the other man was too far gone and missed it. Leyton tried to pass Ben the joint he'd been toking on, but Ben waved it away.

"No thanks."

"So, where's your girl tonight?" said Leyton.

"Drying off."

"Now there's a thought. Go and give her a shout. She was a good laugh, she was."

Leyton took another toke.

"So, are you two serious?"

Ben nodded slowly.

"Yup. Serious."

Crazy watched the exchange carefully. He knew where it was headed, but wanted to see it play out nonetheless.

"Shame," said Leyton. "She's pretty fuckin' hot. Too hot for you mate."

Ben slowly sipped whiskey from his mug, trying like hell to let it slide.

Leyton stared at Ben's Denim clad prosthetic leg.

"So how did you lose yours?"

"I think that's his business," said Crazy. "Don't you?"

"He doesn't mind," said Leyton, "Do you mate? So, what happened? You cut yourself shaving your legs?

Ben took a drag from his glowing cigarette and then flicked it into Leyton's face. He immediately followed it with a fist and caught the surfer square on the jaw, knocking him, and the little camping chair he was wedged into, backwards. Leyton tried to jump up and retaliate, but he couldn't. He was stuck in the chair, on his back, like an upturned turtle pivoting on its shell. Crazy stood up and pushed Ben backwards.

"OK ladies," he said. "Simmer down."

Ben realised the music had stopped now, replaced instead by the slow and steady scratch of the needle against dead vinyl. Crazy motioned with his palms up for both men to wait, while he hovered over the deck to reset the needle. Leyton tried unsuccessfully to lunge at Ben several times. On each attempt he'd try to stand, only to lose his balance and fall back, giggling. The reset record needle picked up the album's first track and Scott started serenading them with the melancholy pantomime of "If You Go Away".

Crazy returned from the turntable and stood toe to toe with Ben, staring him down into submission. The older man watched Ben back down and return to his seat. He then lifted Leyton out of his chair and dusted him down.

"Battling cripples," said Crazy. "I should sell tickets. Now shake hands, or I'll drop both of you."

"Easy old man," said Leyton. "It was just a bit of fun."

The surfer looked at Ben, then slowly extended his open hand. Ben reluctantly reached in to take it. Just as they were about to shake, Leyton jerked forwards and bitch-slapped him in the face. Ben remained still. He just stared at the laughing Aussie, watching him turn away and quickly limp out of there.

Crazy shook his head.

"You know you're turning into a real sweetheart, Leyton."

Leyton lifted up an old red moped that had been left on its side in the grass. He hopped on it and turned the engine over.

"Where are you going now?" said Crazy.

"Down the Cat," said Leyton. "To find some drunks with a sense of style."

"I still got style," Crazy said to himself.

Leyton's moped whined and strained and he pulled away. The remaining two men watched his red taillight buzz away into the darkness like an angry insect and then disappear. Ben and Crazy sat down again. Crazy sighed and topped their drinks up.

"Don't worry," he said. "The little prick won't remember any of it in the morning."

"Do you mind if I just sit here for a bit?" said Ben.

Crazy eyed him. Then a faint smile played across his craggy features, and he nodded. Ben stared up into the night sky. The clouds were breaking. Beyond them, the blackness hung heavy with the weight of hundreds of bright stars. Crazy followed his gaze and found an almost instant sense of peace and relief up there too. Both men smoked and drank and watched the stars in silence.

It was later, when the fire had burned down to just glowing embers, and a harsh, cold wind stirred through the camp, that Ben decided to finally speak. He and Crazy were both slumped in their stretched deckchairs, staring into the last of the fire.

"I lost my wife in a car accident," he said. "It was my fault."

Crazy reached over and drained the last of the bottle into Ben's mug. He gestured towards the false leg.

"Yeah," said Ben. "My permanent little reminder. I got off light. Real light."

Ben smiled, but it was a smile as hollow as the prosthetic leg that supported him.

"I never thought there would be anyone else. And then...then there was Jo.

"So?" said Crazy.

"I got a second chance and I'm screwing it up," said Ben. "I can't let us work, I can't let her be."

"Meaning what? Talk straight man."

"I can't relax. What she does, where she goes, who she talks to. She's on my mind, all the time. It's like there's some kind of threat all around us. And it's my one purpose in life to save her."

"Save her from what?"

"Everything. I just can't chill out. I can't let her live, and it's killing us."

"So, you're carrying a ton of guilt," said Crazy. "I'm afraid there's no medication, no magic remedy for that. You've just got to suck it up and give each day the best you've got."

Ben drained his drink and mulled this over, as the last pockets of fire crackled and died.

"I'm making her nuts you know," he said. "I can see it. She's cheated on me once already. I'll probably drive her to it again."

Crazy began a dry laugh that eventually cracked into a coughing fit.

"What's so funny?" said Ben.

"That's what we do," said Crazy. "We drive them crazy, and they give it back to us in spades. That's the way it works. The way it's always worked."

"Are you married?" said Ben.

"Sure," said Crazy. "This is just my weekend pad when I'm singing at the Cat. I spend the rest of my time painting my white picket fence and drinking daiquiris with my other half on our terrace. No, I'm divorced, like most sane people my age."

"What went wrong?"

"Oh, you know, everything. I picked her up when I was on tour. She was a waitress with big ambitions and a cheap streak a mile wide. We were made for each other. She believed in me. She thought I was going places. I wasn't."

"You made it here."

"No, I got stuck here, there's a difference."

Crazy stared at the ground. He looked up again at Ben and sighed a trail of smoke into the air."

"Listen," he said. "Sweetwater is...a strange place."

"It sure is that."

Now it was Ben's turn to stare into space, the whiskey and emotions of the day having taken their toll.

"I love her you know," he said.

Crazy saved his words for another time. He drained his mug and then leant over to nudge Ben.

"Go to your lady," he said.

"Huh?"

"What are you doing getting drunk with an old fart like me, when you've got a good thing waiting for you in a warm bed?"

"But what do I say to her?"

"Just put one foot in front of the other and keep walking. You'll figure it out by the time you get there."

Ben looked at the old man and started to sober up a little. He stood and smiled at Crazy.

"Thanks man. Really."

As Ben turned to leave, Crazy stood too and grabbed his arm.

"Listen, you're a decent guy and I can see you've had it rough."

The old man seemed to be struggling to find the right words.

"Don't hang around here longer than you have to. OK? Sweetwater's trouble waiting to happen."

Crazy's look was earnest, and Ben saw a great sadness wash over the man after his words came out.

Ben nodded and left.

CHAPTER EIGHT

Ben opened the door to the caravan and crept inside to find it in darkness. He pulled his damp clothes off and used Jo's towel to dry himself, taking the time to sober up and focus his mind. He felt his way across the unfamiliar terrain of the caravan's interior and found the bedclothes. He pulled them back and lay there quietly in the dark, now aware that Jo was awake, though perfectly still.

"I'm sorry," he said eventually.

"No," said Jo. "I was acting up again today. I'm sorry."

Jo sat up and switched on the bedside lamp. Her cheeks were puffy and wet with tears.

"I'm sorry I made you like this," she said. "If I could take back what I did to you, then I would. But I can't, Ben."

He leaned in closer and wiped a fresh tear away.

"Don't cry, baby, please."

"Why can't we just let ourselves be happy?" she said.

Ben took both her hands in his and held them tightly.

"You didn't make me like this. I was already so fucked up when we met, but you still saw something in me worth the risk. I was the one that dragged you into my world, my fears. And I was the one that pushed you into what happened. When I'm calm and lucid I see that, and I know that you still love me."

The two lovers stared at each other.

"I'm nothing without you Jo. If I ever lost you..."

Ben's face darkened at the very thought of this. It wasn't a line. He knew, despite all that they'd been through, he'd be damned without her by his side.

"I'll do anything to make this work," he said. "Fuck the jealousy. Fuck the drinking. Fuck the past. It's all gone, as of now. New slate, new us."

"You promise?"

"I promise. In fact..."

Ben straightened up and released the sliver chain and cross from around his neck.

"Let's make this a proper pact. I hereby promise to stop being stupid and jealous all the time. And you get this as security on my word..."

Ben draped the cross around Jo's neck and fastened it. He then unhooked her surfboard pendant dangling there and tied it around his own neck.

Straight swap.

"And I'll take this as a token that you promise to keep on loving me, and never leave me. Deal?"

"Mmm. Suits you."

"Cheeky bitch. Deal?"

"Deal."

"Come here."

Ben drew Jo in close for a kiss, but at the last minute she resisted him and pulled back.

"You mean it this time?" she whispered.

"I swear on my life," he said.

Satisfied, Jo leant in and they sealed the deal, sharing a deep, but tender kiss. Ben stretched across the bed and turned out the light, failing to notice Irma's mask of pale make-up in the darkness outside their window.

*

Bright sunlight gradually edged its way up over Ben and Jo's faces to warm their skin and sting their eyes. Ben squinted and rolled over, instinctively burying his face in the pillow. Jo lazily shielded her eyes with her hand, then slowly opened them. She took a moment to let her pupils adjust to the sun's glare, then sat up.

"My God," she said. "The sun's actually shining. This has got to be a good sign."

"Shhh," said Ben, his face still deep in the pillow. "My head."

Jo frowned at the back of his head for a moment, before thumping him with her own pillow."

*

Irma's face, still covered in last night's dried layer of cracked foundation and eye make-up, pressed up against the office window. Her wide eyes tracked Ben as he followed Jo through the trailer park gate and out on to the road.

Ben groaned as they made heavy work of the uphill walk into Sweetwater.

"We'll get you a bottle of water in town baby," said Jo. "Serves you right though, you know."

Ben flashed her a dirty look, but he couldn't maintain it. The steep incline, heat and hangover were combining to really take it out of him. Jo sighed and dropped a few steps behind him to rub the back of his neck.

*

Ben stared at the space where his beloved Camper van used to be. The cannibalized shell that now sat in Lonesome's workshop bore no resemblance to the vehicle they were driving two days ago. Jo continued to rub his back in soothing, circular motions in an attempt to keep his rising temper at bay. Lonesome was oblivious to their obvious stress. He mumbled something mechanical and in depth that Ben didn't catch properly, because the older man slurped on a toffee as he talked, constantly circling around the van, brandishing one stripped part, then another. Ben's eyes roamed across the vast array of extracted components scattered over the workshop floor. His gaze finally settled on a pair of brand-new, expensive-looking Nike trainers that Lonesome was wearing. Somehow Ben didn't think they went with the greasy overalls that hadn't been changed since the first time they met him. Ben looked up from his thoughts to see Lonesome's face right in front of him.

"...Quite a bit longer," said the mechanic.

"What?" said Ben, slightly dazed.

"I said, as you can see, it's going to take a bit longer."

"How much longer?"

"Well now, it would take me the rest of today and all of tomorrow just to put it back together again, wouldn't it? So, I reckon we're talking two days minimum. More like three."

"And tell me again," said Ben. "Why you dismantled our Camper van?"

"Well, I haven't worked on this model before. I need to see what makes her tick before I go diving in there, don't I?"

Ben rubbed his face and turned away in frustration, as Lonesome began to weigh up two different sized oil pumps in his hands.

"So, listen, Lonesome," said Jo. "Three days tops for our van back, in one piece, and the original damage repaired. Right?"

Lonesome didn't look up, he was still distracted by the oil pumps. "Yeah, sure."

"And how much is that going to cost us?" said Jo.

Lonesome finally raised his head and looked her in the eye.

"Does it matter?" he said. "It's not like you've got anywhere else to go now, is it?"

Ben sighed in frustration and limped out of the workshop before his temper got the better of him. Jo and Lonesome stared at each other a while longer. The mechanic didn't give an inch. *So that's how it is*, thought Jo. She finally turned and followed Ben out.

Ben rolled a cigarette and lit it, as they strolled back towards Sweetwater in silence. He took long drags and looked at the high street up ahead. The sunshine did nothing to improve the appearance of the town. If anything, the bright daylight only served to further highlight the many cracks visible in the tumbledown row of failed businesses and derelict guesthouses. He exhaled more smoke with a sigh.

"Three more days in Eerie Indiana," said Jo.

Ben grumbled something under his breath.

"Hey," she continued. "You know we'll probably look back on this as the funniest part of the trip."

"Really?"

"Well maybe the bit we tell the most stories about anyway."

Ben's droll, hungover expression was an unimpressed photo-fit of Bob Mitchum and Bill Murray. A cigarette hung from his tired features to labour the point.

"Seriously, I bet you," said Jo.

Ben stared at her for a moment, thought about replying, but then thought better of it.

They walked on and soon reached Olander's general store. Olander's dust covered shop window was plastered with faded trade cards and handwritten notes and adverts. Most of the dated ads showed property for sale. Ben peered in through a clear section of glass, cupping his hand against his own reflection.

"Looks like we've got a live one," he said. "Well, almost."

They pushed through the front door, triggering the quaint tinkle of an old shop bell. Inside, the slight old lady who had crossed their path in town the day before was sitting behind a cash register at the counter. She looked up over her reading glasses from her TV guide and smiled at Jo. Her expression changed to a cold, mistrusting glare when she saw Ben. He nodded a greeting anyway, then quickly stepped behind the rows of tinned goods to escape her gaze. Jo ran her fingers across the tins, wiping a trail in the thick layer of dust that seemed to cover everything in the store. Ben looked around, but he couldn't find any fresh produce; everything here was tinned and prepackaged, and all of the labels on the goods were faded and out of date.

"Still hungry?" whispered Jo.

Ben looked over the top of the shelves to see Mrs. Olander still staring at him. For a moment, he imagined the old woman might have heard Jo's comment, and he flushed red beneath her gaze. Jo carefully selected the two best looking tins of tomatoes, a bag of papyrus-like pasta and some kind of vague tinned meat. She looked at Ben for approval, but he just shrugged. Jo approached the counter with the goods, followed reluctantly by Ben.

"Hi," said Jo.

"Hello dear," said Mrs. Olander, sounding softer than she looked. "Are you enjoying your stay?"

"Yes thanks, it's delightful."

Ben looked down at the shop counter. The TV guide she'd been reading was more than two years out of date. Somehow he wasn't surprised.

"Have you been over to see my Billy yet?"

"No," said Jo, unsure who Billy was supposed to be.

"Billy's my son," said Mrs. Olander. "He runs all the local fishing trips. They're very reasonable."

"Sounds great," said Jo.

Mrs. Olander slid off her chair and tottered around the counter, taking off her apron. Ben shot Jo a concerned look, wondering where this was going.

"Now let me see," said the old woman. "Yes, you're in luck, he's not busy today, I reckon he can fit you in."

"Hang on a minute," said Ben.

"Come on," said Mrs. Olander, ignoring him. "I'll drive you both over there now."

The old lady moved quickly for her age and was at the door before they knew what was happening. She turned the shop sign over to read "Closed" and stood there waiting, with the door wide open.

"Tell me we're not falling for this hard sell," whispered Ben.

"Got any better offers?" said Jo.

"Come on," said Mrs. Olander. "We're not all on holiday, some of us have got a living to earn."

Ben looked at Jo again, this time with pleading eyes.

"What about the groceries?" said Ben.

"Keep the basket," said Mrs. Olander. "I'll ring them up later and add them to your fishing trip bill."

"Really?" said Ben, his eyes boring into Jo.

"Listen, I'm not hanging around this dump doing nothing for the next three days," said Jo. "And the only way I'm going in that sea, is on a boat. Besides, it's a beautiful day."

Ben knew when he was beat. His shoulders slumped as he relented, and he reluctantly followed Jo out through the shop doorway.

CHAPTER NINE

Mrs. Olander's face quickly soured behind the wheel of her Beetle. Despite the absence of any other cars on the road, the old woman drove and acted aggressively in the little car. She jabbed with the gear stick, crunching through gear changes, and habitually left braking and turning until the last possible moment, then stamped on the brakes or wrenched the steering wheel sharply. It made for an exhilarating ride. From the back it seemed to Ben that the little old lady could barely see over the top of the Beetle's dashboard, and he wondered if her tight expression and late reactions were the result of her straining to see the road. Jo sat next to Mrs. Olander in the passenger seat, looking more than a little worried by her driving, but trying not to show it. Ben caught her bracing her knees and hands against the car's interior, as they lurched back and forth.

"He's not just a fisherman you know," said Mrs. Olander, seemingly unaware of the chaos she was causing.

"My Billy's what they call an entrepreneur. Let's see, there's the fishing, the cannery, and the tourist trips." She turned to wink at Jo, before making the Beetle swerve.

"He also sells ornaments. They're very unusual and they're a real steal. I keep telling him he prices everything too low. You'll see when you get there."

"And this is your son, you say?" said Ben.

The old lady scowled at him in the rear-view mirror.

"Of course, he's my son," she said. "Who do you think I've been talking about all this time?"

Ben looked away, out through the window at the ocean, grumbling under his breath.

The battered Beetle picked its way down the jagged coast, towards Bill Olander's tired looking jetty and ramshackle boathouse. A large, abandoned looking cannery, fashioned from sheets of rusting corrugated metal sat a little further along the coast from the boathouse. Screeching gulls gathered and flapped wildly above the churning sea around the jetty in a feeding frenzy. A solitary old fishing boat, a forty-footer, bobbed about on the choppy waters, farting black clouds of smoke from its tired chugging engine. The Beetle pulled up outside the jetty, as sea spray exploded over the rocks ahead of it.

Jo and Ben unfolded themselves out of the car, both looking drained after the journey.

"Make sure you tell him I sent you," called Mrs. Olander. She then gunned the Beetle's engine and spun it around, roaring off back towards town in a shower of spitting gravel.

"Of course," said Ben. "You're on commission aren't you, you old witch."

He and Jo both looked out at the creaking, wooden boathouse and the crashing waves beyond. The structure appeared fragile against the might of the sea. It seemed to lean and shift under duress from each inbound wave. Ben turned to Jo and raised an eyebrow, but she was already walking along the jetty towards it.

"C'mon," she said. "It'll make a man of you."

Ben narrowed his eyes and trailed after her. Each rotten board covering the jetty that led to the boathouse groaned and gave alarmingly under Ben's weight. A large shadow crawled up over his features and he looked up to see the sun disappearing behind grey clouds. He looked down again, through the wide cracks in the jetty, at the swirling waters beneath them. The swell there was cold and violent. Jo reached the boathouse first and disappeared inside through an open door there. Ben followed her with a growing sense of anxiety. He paused and lingered in the doorway, as if teetering on the edge of some unseen threshold. His eyes slowly tracked around the interior of the boathouse, taking in the mass of collected jumble strewn across the floor and walls. Assorted ropes, fishing lines, nets, paddles, life jackets, rods, winches, crates, tools, beer cans and floats all jockeyed for space with dozens and dozens of bleached shark jaws, which were mounted all around the building. Some of the larger, more impressive specimens were carefully suspended from the walls with an obvious reverence, while others just lay around abandoned, dumped on workbenches, mixed up with dirty overalls. Ben looked at Jo. She was staring at the collection in awe.

"Looks like this is where old sharks come to die," she said.

"Don't you think we should've knocked?" said Ben.

"I'm going to check up there," she said, ignoring him. "See if anyone's about."

Jo climbed up a rickety ladder and disappeared on to the boathouse's mezzanine level, before Ben had a chance to complain. He walked in and bent down to examine a huge set of bleached tiger shark jaws. They were armed with multiple rows of serrated, razor-sharp teeth. He slowly leaned in for a closer look, grimly fascinated to see the instruments of death at close range. He tried not to imagine those little daggers scissoring through his flesh.

"I think we should leave," called Ben. "This Billy looks a bit...unbalanced."

Ben's ears then tuned into a distant bubbling sound. He straightened up and limped over to the other side of the room to investigate. He found a large, open vat of boiling water there, its surface thick with a film of rendered fat. He edged closer for a better look.

A sudden thud made Ben flinch and straighten up. He looked around to see a machete embedded in the adjacent wooden work counter, wobbling back and forth. A shadow fell across his face as a large, burly man advanced on him. The middle-aged man's face was craggy, weather-beaten and inscrutable, and his cold blue eyes had a vacant stare. Ben couldn't tell if there was aggression behind those eyes or just indifference. He glanced down at the approaching man's overalls and rubber apron. They were both slick with blood and fish guts. The man quickly closed in, bearing down on him like a rockslide.

Ben backtracked as fast and as far as he could, right up against the cauldron of scalding fat.

"I can't see him," called Jo.

"Down here," shouted Ben.

Ben and Olander both looked up, as Jo peeked over the edge of the mezzanine level's banister.

"Mr. Olander?" she said.

Bill Olander returned a curt nod and grunt.

"Your mom said you might be able to take us out today."

"Fishing?" said Olander.

"Yeah," said Jo.

There was something both obtuse and brutish about the expression on the man's face. Ben still couldn't work out if he was slow, or just naturally aggressive. Then Olander's broad, ruddy face slowly turned to Ben again. A smile gradually creased along the fault line of the fisherman's mouth, as he realized there was money to be made.

*

Ben and Jo sat aboard Olander's fishing boat, The Lady Ann, both bundled up in bright orange life jackets. They were only half a mile out, with the coastline still in plain sight, but the strong waves here rolled them around like marbles. Ben already had a greenish tinge about him and the focused expression of a man trying to hang on to his breakfast. Jo seemed unaffected by the choppy seas. She watched with excitement, as Olander emerged from the cabin with a white bucket and made straight for the stern. The fisherman dug a trowel into the bucket with a meaty squelch. When he pulled it out again it was bright red. He grinned at Ben and leant over the side, as he proceeded to chum the water.

"Don't worry," he said. "It won't be long. Not in these waters."

Olander kept his eyes on Ben, as he shoveled the chum overboard.

Sadistic, thought Ben. *That's it. This guy's a sadist.* Then his next thought was one of panic as he felt the contents of his stomach quickly rise.

"Looks like there's something wrong with your man," said Olander, grinning.

Jo glanced over at Ben, but he'd already turned away with his hand over his mouth. He leaned over the side, unable to hold back any longer.

"I wouldn't let him do that if I was you," said Olander.

Jo smiled for a moment, then realized the fisherman wasn't joking. She quickly pulled Ben back from the edge and stared grimly into the waves.

*

A dark slick of chummed water trailed far behind The Lady Ann, as she bobbed about under grey skies off the coast of Sweetwater. Olander stood at the stern, looking out to sea proudly, and yet somehow blankly, surveying the horizon for some unspoken sign. Ben, having finally found his sea legs, along with a sense of apathy, smoked and looked at the horizon too. Though his was a look of boredom, cut with slight worry, as he watched dark clouds gather where the sun had once been. Even Jo's enthusiasm seemed to have waned, though her eyes remained fixed on the ocean too. Olander caught their expressions and frowned. He marched off into the cabin and returned moments later with two large fishing rods and large coil of rope.

"Fishing around here's easy," he said. "It's not like those dead waters further up the Bight. Here, you just bait and wait."

Olander motioned for both of them to stand. He then handed them a fishing rod each.

"Say, would you folks like to try out my new tourist thing? Maybe let me know if you like it before the season starts?"

Jo saw Ben's face crease, as if he was trying to swallow away a bad taste.

"Obviously, today's trip would be on the house if you did…"

Ben looked at Olander for a moment, then at Jo. There was a big, hopeful smile swelling on her face. He turned back to the fisherman and reluctantly nodded. Olander grinned at him and lifted up the rope. Then, in one swift, fluid movement, he slipped it over Ben and pulled it up tight across his chest and under his arms. Ben dropped the rod and stared at Olander with a stunned expression. Olander paused, and for a second, Jo and Ben made eye contact and swapped confused looks.

Maybe this was a joke, thought Ben.

But then Olander grabbed hold of Ben with both hands and ran him to the stern, throwing him head-first over the side and into the water. Olander then calmly turned to face Jo. Her eyes were wide and uncomprehending.

"Yep," said Olander. "The fishing here's real easy. The real trick though is to haul your catch out of the water before everything else down there takes a bite out of it."

Ben broke the surface of the freezing cold waves. He snorted away the salt water that had flooded his throat and sinuses, but he was still left with a thick, deafening sound rushing through his ears. He wiped his hair out of his face and opened his eyes. Panic was already setting in. He made sharp, scared about-turns, revolving in the water, quickly scanning the surrounding sea for threat. He saw blood in the water all around him, and realized he was slap bang in the middle of the chum trail.

"Oh God," he whispered. "Oh God."

His hands instinctively reached for the rope lassoed tightly around his chest. He glanced up at the stern of The Lady Ann. The fishing boat was already drifting away from him. He saw Jo lean over the boat's edge. She was shouting something at him with a terrified expression.

There was no sign of Olander.

Ben treaded water and shook his head from side to side. A sudden plunging sound rushed through his ears and popped hard, as he felt his sinuses clear. He could then hear Jo screaming at him.

"Swim!" she shouted. "For fuck's sake, swim!"

Ben tracked the eye line from her horrified expression and quickly spun around a hundred and eighty degrees in the water. A wave of saltwater smacked directly into his face disorienting him. He coughed, spat and wiped it away from his eyes.

Then he saw it.

A huge dorsal fin broke the surface of the blooded waters less than eighty feet away. He watched it cut towards him, closing in on his direction. Then it sank below the waves. Ben continued to stare straight ahead, his whole-body shivering. He caught a last glimpse of the pointer, as its dark tail flicked at the water and it dived under.

"Swim Ben!" shouted Jo. "Quick, swim!"

Ben suddenly spasmed against the water, as he broke out of his trance. He immediately turned and pushed himself forwards against the current, throwing arm over arm, trying to drag his dead leg back to The Lady Ann. His shivering breaths came harder and faster, as the thump of pumping blood and rushing water filled his ears.

Then he stopped.

Sensing he was out of time, he slowly turned on the spot, expecting to see the trailing predator closing in at any moment.

But there was nothing.

Ben floated there like fish-food on the surface, as confusion flooded his stressed brain and prevented him from trying to escape. He slowly lowered his head and peered down into the dark depths beneath his feet. His stomach turned over and over with the vertiginous sense of someone standing on the edge of a precipice, staring down into the abyss. His eyes grew wide, as they began to make out a contrast moving in the depths below him; taking shape. It was a hulking dark mass with a ghostly white underbelly charging up to greet him. He watched in horror as the breaching pointer's jaws opened wide and its black eyes rolled over white, preparing to bite.

A whipping sound sliced through the air towards him, and suddenly he was being hauled backwards at great speed, with foaming water crashing into his face. The Lady Ann powered along at full throttle, as Ben was keelhauled behind it, skiing through the surf like a speeding lure. It was all Ben could do to hold his breath and nerve, as he rushed headlong through the water, expecting to feel a hundred sharp teeth slice through his torso at any moment.

Just as suddenly, the violent, rushing water dropped away to nothing and Ben slowed and floated to a halt. He bobbed around on the surface for a moment, before he managed to open his eyes and focus on Olander watching him from the stern of The Lady Ann.

"How was it?" called the fisherman.

Ben frowned at him in cold confusion. He swallowed and tried to get his bearings. He then saw Olander jump up and run back to the bridge in a hurry.

Ben was jerked back into sudden awareness of his predicament, He tried to scream, but couldn't. He forced himself to look around, just in time to see the huge dorsal fin of the great white approaching again.

Fast.

Ben instinctively tried to gulp in air, knowing what was coming next, but it was too late. Again, he was snatched away and hauled along by the taught rope, rushing headlong through the water, gasping for breath.

This second burst of keelhauling lasted much longer than the first, as Olander gunned the fishing boat's engine and steered one way, then another, in a desperate attempt to shake off the pursuing shark. Ben felt himself being thrown about from left to right, and back again, as he rode through The Lady Ann's wake and more and more waves smacked into him.

When Olander finally cut the engines and circled around to pick Ben up, he was barely conscious. Ben floated upright, with his eyes closed, his face just above the waterline. He was too exhausted to panic or scream, but he felt a silent terror swell deep inside, as he waited in agony and counted the seconds to the moment he would be dragged from the water. Finally, after what seemed like an eternity, The Lady Ann appeared alongside, and Olander and Jo hauled his sodden, bedraggled form aboard.

Olander handed Jo a thick blanket, which she wrapped around Ben. She rubbed his body vigorously through it to warm him up and stop him slipping into shock, but he was a shivering wreck. Olander stood next to them, watching, waiting impatiently.

"Well?" said Olander. "What do you reckon? I was thinking about all those extreme sports fellas. I reckon they'd go a bundle on it, don't you?"

Jo turned and stared at Olander with raw, naked fury. The fisherman just stared back, almost innocently, seemingly bemused by her hostility.

"You're always reading about them," Olander said. "Jumping off this, crashing into that. Well, this would be right up their street, eh? What do you think?"

Ben slowly raised his shell-shocked features to stare at Olander, still struggling to keep his shaking under control.

"I think," he said. "You're going to need a faster boat."

Olander stared at him in confused concentration, trying to digest the comment for meaning. Seemingly beaten, the fisherman just frowned and raised his eyes to the dark, foreboding sky brewing above their heads.

"We better head in," he said. "Looks like there's a storm coming."

"Another storm," said Ben, still shivering. "Of course there is."

CHAPTER TEN

The sky was full and black with the promise of rain by the time Olander's battered pick-up pulled into the trailer park. Jo helped Ben out of the vehicle. He was still sodden and wrapped in the same blanket she'd given him on The Lady Ann. Jo glared at Bill Olander and slammed the pick-up's door shut on him, but the fisherman still seemed oblivious to her anger and the gesture just bounced off him. He turned and waved a hello to Crazy and Leyton, who both sat on orange crates outside Irma's office playing cards. Leyton eyed Ben and then the heavy clouds gathering above their heads.

"How the hell did you get wet this time?" he said. "It ain't even rained yet."

Jo tightened the blanket around Ben and ushered him away before he could reply. As they walked away, Ben turned and saw that Olander was out of the pick-up. He was standing opposite Crazy, giving the older man a cold stare. He then noticed Leyton turn to stare at the old man too; the surfer's features suddenly appearing stony, rather than stoned. Ben kept watching and saw Irma's painted face appear at the office window too; a third hostile look aimed at Crazy. He saw the old man shuffle and fidget uncomfortably, starting to buckle under the weight of the stares. Crazy caught Ben's eye and looked embarrassed. The old man coughed and stood up, pushing past Olander and Leyton to catch up with Ben and Jo. Crazy nodded a greeting to them and helped walk Ben back to their caravan. Crazy glanced back to see Leyton and Olander still watching him. When he turned back, Crazy saw Ben frowning at him.

"Sorry," said Crazy, a little too quickly. "I should've warned you about Olander. You both OK?"

"Not really," said Ben. "You got any of that whiskey left?"

"Sure," said Crazy. "I'll bring a bottle over."

Jo gave Ben a worried look, but quickly decided this wasn't the time to challenge him on his drinking.

"I was actually hoping you two might want to join me and Leyton down at The Cat tonight," said Crazy.

Ben noticed something different about the old man today. There was an awkwardness to him at odds with the reckless, my-way-or-the-highway bravado he'd projected the day before.

"I'm singing," continued Crazy. "It ain't Caesars Palace, but I thought you might enjoy it."

"Ben's had a really rough day," said Jo. "I think we better rest up."

"It's a short set," said Crazy. "I'll even throw in a couple of rounds on me."

"No thanks Crazy," said Jo. "We'd better..."

"We'll be there," said Ben, cutting in. "We just need a little rest and a shower first."

Jo's eyes flashed with anger, but she held her breath as they reached the caravan. Crazy supported Ben while she fumbled for the key and opened the caravan door. She quickly disappeared inside without a word. The two men watched her go and then looked at each other.

"Looks like you might be in the doghouse," said Crazy.

"She'll be OK.

The two men lingered there and for a moment, Ben saw a sadness and appreciation in the older man's eyes that touched him. It suddenly dawned on him that it was a huge deal for a man like Crazy to ask them to come and watch him perform. A man who had obviously failed, yet still proudly believed in himself; believed he still had something to give.

"Look," said Crazy. "Maybe you shouldn't come tonight. You do look pretty banged up. I just, I just had to ask."

"It's OK," said Ben. "We'll be there."

"No, you don't look so good."

"I said we'll be there," said Ben. "Now if you're still offering, I could really use that drink."

"OK."

"OK."

Crazy then helped Ben inside the caravan and left him to Jo.

Jo was quiet, too quiet. Ben watched her fill the kettle and pull two mugs out of the cupboard. He thought about his request for Crazy's whiskey and his promise to go to The Black Cat, all straight after the strange events on The Lady Ann. He knew Jo was angry with him and that a storm was brewing in the caravan every bit as destructive as the one churning in the sky outside. He stared at the boiling kettle, trying to think of something to say that might lighten her mood. She had over filled it and the water quickly began to bubble over, the lid flipping and juddering, as it rode the steam's building pressure. She put two spoons of sugar in Ben's mug with a shaking hand, then filled it with hot water. She began stirring the tea automatically.

"Are you all right?" he said.

"I'm fine," she said, still stirring. "You're the one that came this close to dying."

"Maybe you should sit down."

"Is it me," she said, "Or did that bloody boat trip not happen?"

She turned and looked at him. He could see she was fraught, strung out.

"I thought you were going to be ripped apart in front of my eyes," she said. "And I made you go out there."

"You didn't make me do anything."

"How come you're so fucking calm?" Her voice was wavering now.

"I don't know," he said. "I'm tired, and I guess I'm just glad to be alive."

Jo turned away and snatched the spoon from his mug of tea. She frowned.

"Fuck. You don't even take sugar."

She tipped the tea down the sink and sniffed, as her eyes began to well up. Ben moved in and closed his arms around her, as she started to cry.

"I nearly lost you," she said. "I nearly lost you."

He remained there, hugging her tightly, as she bawled into his chest.

Crazy rapped on the door and opened it. He saw the two of them embracing as she sobbed. Ben caught his eye and Crazy nodded at him, putting a half-full bottle of whiskey on the work-surface. Crazy then carefully retreated, closing the door behind him as quietly as he could.

Crazy stood outside Ben's caravan, staring into space. He swallowed hard, trying to reconcile his feelings of guilt and defiance wrestling inside. He thought about the couple, about this man and what he'd been through. He thought about what was yet to come. Something in Crazy snapped and he about-turned sharply. He reached for the caravan's door handle again, but before he could turn it, a woman's wrinkled hand closed over his. Crazy turned to see Irma standing next to him, her insane dark eyes shining at him from that painted face. He hesitated, but kept his hand on the handle. Irma stared at him and slowly shook her head. She then opened her mouth as wide as it would stretch, revealing a lolling, severed stump where her tongue used to be.

Crazy stared at the severed tongue in disgust. He withdrew his hand from the door and backed away from Irma and her mouth. He reluctantly retreated in the direction of his own caravan.

Message received and understood.

Irma closed her mouth and continued to stare blankly at him as he walked away.

*

Jo and Ben slept through the rest of the afternoon and well into the evening. She lay in his arms, in the darkness. It would have been a peaceful scene, except for Ben's eyes dancing and rolling beneath their lids, as he replayed the same nightmare that awaited him every time he closed his eyes. He moaned and his face tightened, as if in pain, as he watched the car crash play out in his mind yet again; the day his wife was taken from him. It was the same dream, countless times; again and again, always the same.

His eyes snapped open.

For a moment, he stared deep into the shadows of the darkened room, through them. His brow creased in confusion, as he tried to fully emerge from his memories. He slowly unraveled himself from Jo, making her murmur, and crawled to the edge of the bed. There, cast in a moonlit glow, he rolled a cigarette and stared out through the window at nothing. A light tapping on the caravan's door roused him from his introspection.

"Yeah?" he said quietly.

The door opened to reveal Crazy. The old man was squeezed into a showy, black tuxedo that had seen better days.

"Are you still coming?" He whispered.

Jo groaned and turned over, burying her head beneath the pillows. Ben coughed, as a wave of Crazy's aftershave hit him.

"What is that, eau de mace?" he said. "Yeah, give us ten minutes."

"I'm driving," said Crazy. "You'll be sharing with Leyton, so no more fist fights, OK?"

"Don't worry about me," said Ben. "I've had enough drama for one day."

Crazy half-smiled and turned to leave.

"Hey Crazy," said Ben.

The old man stopped tond turned to face him.

"You look like a real pro."

Crazy's mouth stretched into a wide grin before he could stop himself. He opened his mouth to speak, then just blinked something away from his eyes instead, and quickly turned away on his heels, shutting the door behind him. Ben moved over to the bed and raised a pillow to reveal a snug and drowsy Jo beneath, complete with wild sleep-hair. He leaned in and kissed her forehead. She slowly opened her eyes and gazed up at him. He felt the last echoes of fear and guilt from the dream finally melt away. He looked into Jo's eyes, and he experienced a brief, but true moment of pure clarity. In that moment he had just one thought. He realized how much he truly loved this woman.

*

Thunder rumbled through apocalyptic skies above, as Crazy's Camira hurtled through the night towards Sweetwater. Crazy was behind the wheel with Leyton beside him, smoking a joint. Jo and Ben sat in the back; Ben unable to take his eyes off the road speeding towards them through the windscreen. Another loud clap of thunder rolled out from the skies overhead.

"The Gods are sure pissed tonight," said Leyton, smirking. "Eh Crazy?"

The older man stared ahead and said nothing.

"What's the matter with you?" said Leyton. "Stage fright?"

The surfer turned back to speak to Jo, his eyes getting lost on the way and finding her legs instead of her face.

"Believe me, it ain't him that needs to be afraid. It's the audience."

"I'm sure you're going to be great, Crazy," said Jo.

"C'mon old timer," said Leyton, sarcastically. "You're not normally so jumpy. After all, you played Vegas. Apparently."

Leyton then leaned in close to Crazy and whispered in his ear, all traces of humor suddenly gone.

"Lighten the fuck up," said the surfer.

Crazy looked back at Leyton, but still said nothing.

The Camira pulled up in town, and its four passengers stepped out into a street as black as the night sky. All the streetlamps were out tonight. The only source of light was radiating from the Black Cat's sign and doorway. Ben turned his collar against the wind and looked up, as more rumbles of low thunder growled above. Jo and Ben shared a glance, as they steeled themselves for Sweetwater's nightlife. They followed Crazy and Leyton through the seedy looking doorway, into the bar known as The Black Cat.

CHAPTER ELEVEN

It was obvious from its rough, nautical-themed interior, that The Black Cat was a watering hole every bit as predatory as the seas along Sweetwater's coastline. The bar had very basic wooden furniture, bearing the scars of dozens of raucous bar fights. Pieces of driftwood and upended barrels had been recycled to create the bar's tables and chairs, in a basic, functional way, rather than for a hip effect. Ben eyed the smoke-stained walls draped with fishing nets and decorated with sets of bleached shark jaws; no doubt caught locally. Some insane, old-school jazz was unraveling from the jukebox, as he looked around and found hostile stares from the other patrons of The Black Cat, each drinking in their own isolated pockets around the room.

Ben and Jo followed Crazy and Leyton to the bar. Crazy ordered the drinks, while Ben continued to check out the faces gathered for tonight's performance. There were about thirty other people in the room, a lot more than Ben would've guessed were still living in Sweetwater. He recognized Olander first, staring at him from a table in the corner where he was sat with his mother. Irma sat alone at another table toying with a sherry, her thick make-up plastered on as always. She flashed him a disturbing grin, which he did his best to return. Then his eyes settled on Henry and Angie Ho. Angie Ho looked at him with obvious contempt, while her husband aimed his gaze in the opposite direction, clearly giving him the cold shoulder. Ben shrugged and turned back to the bar, as Crazy handed him a whiskey. Leyton took his drink from the old man and left without a word. He made a beeline for an aging blonde in the corner who appeared to be dressed for something livelier than this. Ben watched Crazy talk to the serious looking Maori man who was serving behind the bar. The bartender was dressed in ripped punk gear, revealing that he was ripped too. The Maori was covered with biker style piercings and tattoos and generally looked like bad news. Ben looked away. He was starting to feel self-conscious. It wasn't just that he had the feeling that everyone in the bar was staring at them; he could see that everyone was. It was more that he had the sensation that everyone else might be in on a joke except for him. He held on tightly to Jo and made a point of staring back at the faces scrutinizing them. Crazy leaned towards Ben and raised his glass, toasting it with Ben's, then Jo's.

"A man's got to do what a man's got to do," said Crazy. "So, here's to us men."

"And their better halves," said Jo.

"And their better halves," repeated Crazy.

The three downed their drinks and thudded the empty glasses on to the bar counter.

"I better make a move," said Crazy. "I'm due on."

"Cheer up," said Ben. "I'm sure you'll be great."

Crazy slapped Ben's shoulder. Ben thought he looked awkward again, almost ashamed.

"Yeah..."

Ben watched the old man reluctantly slope towards the microphone, looking more like a condemned man than an entertainer. Ben shook his head, puzzled, and turned back to the bar.

"Same again?" he said to Jo.

"Yeah," she said. "Let's see if we can make this one last a little longer, eh?"

Ben tried repeatedly to catch the bartender's eye, but the Maori deliberately ignored him, even though there was no one else waiting to be served. Ben took out a twenty and held it up. There was no response. Ben shifted position to stand directly in front of the bartender, blocking his view of the stage, but the man just stared past him with bored, cruel eyes.

"Can I get some drinks please," said Ben.

The bartender finally turned and stared at Ben. He slowly took a cigarette out, lit it and exhaled a plume of grey smoke into Ben's face.

The man then poured a large glass of whiskey and proceeded to down it himself. Ben could feel himself shaking. He looked down to see both of Jo's hands pinning his right arm firmly to the bar counter.

"Just another small-town asshole," she whispered. "Let's wait around to watch a couple of Crazy's numbers, then take off. OK?"

Ben looked up to see the bartender goading him, apparently amused that he was being held in check by a woman. He sighed smoke up into the air, then blew Ben a kiss. Ben's fist clenched around the twenty, but Jo held him steady.

"Then I'll take you home," continued Jo. "And show you how much I love you."

Ben held the bartender's taunting stare, until eventually the other man finally broke off eye contact by looking towards the back of the bar. The man then turned away and started fixing drinks. Ben traced his last line of sight across the room to the Ho's table. Ho was busy talking to his wife, holding her hand above the table between his own. Ben's eyes searched beyond Ho until another figure, a little further back slid into focus. A dapper looking man in his early forties wearing a suit sat directly behind Ho. A younger, seductive looking Asian woman in a figure-hugging dress sat next to him, or rather wrapped around him like a snake. Both of them stared at Ben from the back of the room and the man raised his glass to him. The Maori bartender reluctantly slid two more whiskies across the bar towards Ben.

"For the fastest fish in town," he said with a smirk.

Ben tried to hand the bartender his twenty, but the bartender just snorted with contempt and headed to the other end of the counter to dry glasses. Ben looked back at the man in the suit again. The man raised his glass again and tipped it slightly in Ben's direction, before taking a sip.

"Looks like we've pulled," said Jo. "Think we better say hello?"

The lights around the room began to dim and the jazz music on the jukebox faded out, replaced by the low, fuzzy buzz of an old amplifier.

"In a bit," said Ben.

His eyes were fixed on the raised plinth at the other end of the room, now illuminated by a spotlight. This *stage* was empty, but there was a microphone and stand on it.

Ben watched as Crazy, looking every inch the jaded crooner, stepped up on to the makeshift stage, glass in hand, and squinted against the spotlight's glare. Moments later, the light's beam was adjusted to a less severe angle, allowing Crazy to blink and finally find his bearings. A badly worn, instrumental backing track of Ervin Drake's "It was a very good year" filled the room and Crazy began to serenade the bar.

Ben was impressed.

The old man's voice was still up to the task, and he carried the song well. The performance wasn't polished, but it had the genuine weight of one who had loved and lost many times over. Crazy's eyes even appeared to well up, as he appeared to channel his own emotions into the lyrics. Ben looked around the bar at the various silhouettes gathered there and began to wonder if Crazy's emotional outpouring was more than just a performance. Ben and Jo weren't just the only people in The Black Cat listening to Crazy's song; they were the only ones acknowledging his presence at all. The rest of the crowd just carried on drinking and chatting without even looking at Crazy. Ben felt a sudden rush of sadness for the old man standing on the stage, giving it his all. The whole scene was brutal to watch, and it made Ben angry.

Crazy managed to finish the song and Ben made a point of clapping loudly against the sudden vacuum of silence it left in the room. Jo joined in too, but their lone applause only pronounced the sadness of the situation. The house lights snapped back on and Crazy's microphone and backing track were faded down to almost nothing, so that when he launched into "MacArthur's Park", he was demoted to just background muzak for the bar. Crazy stuck it out though, and continued to put his heart into the performance, but the joke was clearly on him.

Ben saw the bartender smirking from behind a small mixing desk on the bar.

"Prick," said Ben.

Crazy soldiered on with the song, despite being ignored by the room again, looking like a man slowly being destroyed, piece by piece. Ben downed his drink and turned to order another, only to see the bartender standing right in front of him with a tray full of whiskies. The Maori stared at him and then nodded towards the back of the room. He then moved off and Ben started after him. Jo grabbed Ben's arm to stop him.

"Come on, baby," she said. "Let's go."

"I just want to see what's going on," said Ben.

Ben and Jo followed the bartender, as he cut his way through the room with his large frame. He led them towards the man in the suit at the back of the bar who paid for their last round. As their destination became apparent, Ben noticed anxious looks coming his way from wide eyes all around the room. He caught sight of Henry Ho shuffling back awkwardly in his chair as they passed by.

"Still here then, eh?" said the old Polynesian.

Ben ignored him and approached his benefactor's table. He made eye contact with the man in the suit, as the bartender put the whole tray of drinks down. There were twenty whiskies in all. The man at the table smiled and gestured for them both to sit, so they did. Ben tried to read the man's face. He appeared serene, maybe drunk, but somehow Ben didn't think so; his eyes looked too sharp, too mean. Ben was aware that the rest of the customers in the bar were watching them. He began to feel like a rabbit sitting down to dinner with a hawk.

"Evening," said the man in the suit.

"Evening," said Ben. "Thanks for the drinks."

"That's OK. It's a close-knit community, it can be a little difficult for strangers to get served in here sometimes."

Ben turned to look at the bartender, but the big man had already disappeared.

"Don't mind Ali," said the man in the suit. "He's got issues."

"Yes, he does," said Ben. "And you are?"

"Dr. Harris," said the man. "And this is my nurse, Kim."

The Asian woman stared at Ben and Jo, and tightened her hold on Harris, coiling around him like a python.

"I'm Ben, and this is Jo."

"I know," said Harris, looking just a little smug and superior.

"So, you're a doctor?" said Jo.

"Sort of," said Harris. "Anyway, I just had to buy a round for the man crazy enough to try Olander's game. That idiot's asked everybody in town. So, bravo to you."

"I didn't really..."

"No," interrupted Harris. "I know you didn't know what you were getting yourself into, but you are still here in one piece, well sort of. Take it from me, considering what's in the waters around here, that's some feat. So, like I said, bravo."

Harris tilted his glass towards Ben. Ben raised his glass too, suspecting he was being mocked, but not sure why exactly. He could still see the faces of all the other locals turned his way, their expressions of anticipation all aimed at Harris's table. The mood was one of fear and curiosity, as they all but held their breath waiting to see what would happen next. He noticed Jo's eyes widen, as the woman sitting next to Harris held their gaze with a playful expression and slowly slid her hand up the inside of the doctor's thigh. Ben tried to ignore the gesture, quickly growing tired of these games.

"So," he said. "Are you some sort of a big deal around here Harris?"

The man shook his head and feigned embarrassment.

"Me, no. Why do you ask?"

"No one here's taken their eyes off this table since we sat down."

Harris flashed him a smug grin.

Ben was really starting to dislike the guy.

"It's not me," said Harris. "It's you. You're the new novelty in town, the man everyone wants to meet."

Ben felt a flush of embarrassment burn through his cheeks. He watched Harris ease back into his chair, still grinning, staring at him with those dangerous blue eyes; another in Sweetwater's parade of sociopaths just spoiling for a fight. He looked over at Kim. She was still staring at Jo, while her hand worked its way up towards Harris's zipper. Harris's gaze shifted to Jo too. He looked her up and down and smiled like a predator.

"Jo, eh?" he said, showing his teeth.

Ben took a moment to compose himself, to make ready for a fight. He started to open his mouth to speak, but Harris pushed a double towards him before he could get the words out.

"Are you game, Ben?" said the doctor.

A drinking competition, thought Ben.

Ben instinctively paused. He looked around the room for help, but found only an audience teetering on the edge of its seat. Even Crazy had now stopped singing, too engrossed by the strange scene unfolding at Harris's table to carry on with the show.

Jo's hand reached for Ben's under the table and squeezed it tightly.

"Please baby," she whispered. "Let's go."

Ben drew strength from her, but her fear also made defiance and bloody mindedness swell up inside him too. He didn't know what Harris's problem was, what his game was. He didn't know why all the good folk of Sweetwater had been on their case from the moment they'd arrived, but he'd had enough. He wasn't walking away now. He wasn't turning his back on another confrontation with one of these pricks, not until he'd stood up to them, not until he'd showed them what he was made of.

Ben fixed his eyes on the doctor as he raised the glass of whiskey.

"Please baby," Jo whispered in his ear. "Don't."

Ben squeezed her hand, then downed the drink in one. He leaned back in his chair and smirked at Harris.

Harris's own grin began to spread further along his features, threatening to split them.

"We have a contender," he said. "I thought you looked like a man who enjoys a drink or two."

"It's what I'm good at," said Ben.

"Very bad for your health though," said Harris. "Don't you worry about your health, Ben?"

"Not anymore."

Ben let go of Jo's hand. He rolled a cigarette and popped it into his mouth, relaxing into the game.

"You want to play, Harris?" he said. "So, let's play."

Jo's fingers, deprived of his hand, clutched at his thigh, her nails digging tightly into the flesh above his prosthesis. Ben blew smoke and leaned forwards to rest his hands on the table.

Enough of this.

He was letting his dark side out tonight.

Harris eyed him coldly and downed his drink. He then turned to French kiss Kim. Ali the barman appeared next to the table and began serving more drinks. He put another full glass down in front of both men. Ben looked at all the doubles grouped in the centre of the table.

A real competition.

"Please Ben," whispered Jo.

Ben said nothing. He stared dead ahead and slowly raised the next glass to his lips. He then dropped his head back and put away the shot, slamming the empty glass down on the table. He took a deep breath, but did his best to hide it. The doctor reached for his whiskey and put it away mechanically. Ali dished out two more drinks and stood back.

"You're a thirsty mother," said Ben. "Aren't you?"

"It's a dry country," said Harris.

"Please Ben," whispered Jo. "You've got nothing to prove to these people, or to me."

Ben listened to the rain hammering against the corrugated roof above their heads; listened to it washing down through the guttering outside. Now that the music had stopped, you could hear a pin drop.

Nothing to prove to them, or to you. But what about myself, he thought.

He sank his double and put the glass down on the table, carefully this time. Harris lifted his drink in response, but then paused.

"I couldn't help but notice your crippled gait as you limped in," he said. "Would you like me to take a look at that for you? Maybe I can help?"

Harris then knocked his drink back, smiling.

Ben reached for his next drink before Ali could set it down. He was sweating now, but not from fear or embarrassment; he was lost to himself, lost to the animal side. The drinking side. The side that felt, rather than thought. The side that acted, rather than talked. The side that fought rather than feared.

Something flashed in the doctor's eyes. Ben guessed it was recognition. After all, deep down they had the same condition, the same demon. He didn't know this man, didn't know his agenda, but he definitely knew *what* he was. He knew that behind their daytime masks of civility, they were both the same kind of self-loathing, asshole drunk.

Ben downed his whiskey and licked his lips, starting to enjoy the game more and more. Jo let go of his leg. She edged her chair further away from him.

Ben barely noticed. His focus was all on Harris now. He was starting to rile the man and he liked it.

Harris tipped his own whiskey down his throat and clicked his fingers. Ali instantly handed him another. He put that one away too.

"This fucking town," said Harris. "Isn't it enough that we have to scrape a living out here, in the middle of nowhere, without turds like you washing up on the beach."

Harris spoke to the room, addressing no one in particular, and not making sense, at least not to Ben anyway.

"Is this the fucking best we can do?" he continued.

The bar was silent, until Henry Ho coughed.

Harris took a deep breath and regained his composure. He ran his fingers back through his lank hair and grinned again, but it was a hollow grin, a fake grin. Ben reached for his next glass, but Jo placed her hand over the top of it.

"Please Ben."

Ben looked at her imploring face. The woman he had been gazing at a few hours ago, the woman he adored and would do anything to protect, the woman he had promised so much to, was now a million miles away from here. All he could see right now was someone else in his way, someone trying to manipulate him, to pull his strings; someone telling him no.

"Please," she said.

"Relax."

There were tears in her eyes.

Always tears, if they couldn't get their own way, if they couldn't control you, he thought.

"You swore it would be different, Ben," she said. "You swore to me."

Ben pretended not to hear. He had to focus on his adversary, and on the next glass in front of him. It wasn't going to drink itself. He tipped his head back and finished it. He then started on his second, to match the doctor's escalation, hardly aware that Jo had left the table.

Ben lined up the next drink and threw his head back again. He savored every drop, as tiny rivulets of stinking whiskey ran from his lips and picked their way down through the growth on his chin. He grimaced, creasing the lines at the corners of his eyes and along the furrow of his scar. He heard some abusive put-down slide out of Harris's lizard like mouth, but the man no longer made sense to him. Ben's head continued to tilt backwards, as he allowed the booze to fill his throat, but he kept going, further and further back, until he finally tipped over. The back of his skull hit the bar floor with a jolt. He could hear people somewhere behind him laughing hard enough to burst blood vessels. He pushed his palms against the floorboards and tried to stand, but his muscles failed him. He saw more grinning faces peer down at him, but only for a moment. Their features quickly softened and became hazy, as everything began to slide out of focus.

CHAPTER TWELVE

Ben slowly opened his dazed eyes and tried to focus them. He was lying on his back on the floor of The Black Cat. He sat up and stared around the room. Everybody was still there, drinking and chatting, carrying on as normal, or at least whatever passed for normal in Sweetwater, seemingly oblivious to the state he was in. He made eye-contact with Henry Ho. The hotelier and sometime peeping tom raised his glass in Ben's direction in some dark, sarcastic toast, an expression of pure contempt written on his face. Ben looked over at Harris's table. The doctor was still there, with his nurse girlfriend, and someone else. Ben blinked. Harris was sat between two women. His Asian girlfriend, Kim.

And Jo.

Ben stared at Jo for some time, making sure his eyes weren't lying to him, but there she was, sitting with them, up close and very personal. Both Jo and Kim looked high to Ben. He watched them conduct their hands all over Harris with vacant sexuality, like bored porn actresses sleepwalking through their roles. Harris reached over and pulled down Jo's top, releasing her breasts. He leaned in over them, lingering there for a moment, before turning to look directly at Ben. Harris grinned at him, then began gorging himself on one of Jo's nipples.

"Bastard," slurred Ben.

He tried to stand, but he felt heavy; unnaturally heavy. He struggled against the strange, invisible, dense weight on him and managed to rise with difficulty, but then felt a sudden, violent tug on his prosthetic leg that pulled him down again. It was so jarring that it took both his legs from underneath him and smashed his head back into the floorboards. Confused, Ben rolled over on to his back and slowly raised his head again. He looked down at his splayed legs and watched, as his prosthetic was jerked and wrenched again by some invisible, violent force. The false leg rose and dragged him along the ground for several feet, then the unseen force let go of him as suddenly as it had attacked.

Ben breathed hard and looked around in a stupor. Everybody else in the bar was watching him and giggling at his predicament. He looked back at Harris's table and saw the doctor smirking at him, as Jo and Kim reached into his trousers with dead hands and even deader stares.

Ben rolled over on to his front and tried to crawl towards Harris's table, but the invisible assailant struck again. He was dragged backwards at speed by something gripping his dead leg, as his fingers tried to find purchase and his nails raked across the wooden floor. He managed to shout for help this time, until the words were smashed out of him by a collision with a barrel-keg-table. The impact was enough to flip him over on to his back again and he groaned, as he was quickly hauled through the bar like a struggling fish caught on a line, now being reeled in.

Ben saw the far wall racing towards him, coming faster and faster, the source of the force pulling him still unclear. He tensed and braced himself for the inevitable impact. Seconds later he crashed through a chair, splintering its legs in the process, then rolled over and over, gathering speed, before slamming sideways into the wall.

Ben groaned and tried to raise his head, but he was disoriented. Something above him caught his attention and he instinctively looked up, just in time to see a wobbling set of bleached shark jaws dislodge from their fitting on the wall after the impact. He watched in a daze, as the jaws broke away and fell silently towards him, razor sharp teeth glistening, as they twisted and turned, tumbling through the air towards his face. Ben screwed his eyes shut and tried to scream, as he heard the sound of dozens of sharp knives thudding into meat.

*

Ben's glassy eyes slowly opened and rolled around the room, but he failed to comprehend anything they showed him. He tried to rise, but felt a dull ache pulse from the back of his head and travel through his body in a wave. He fell back on to the bed and into another deep sleep.

When he eventually awoke again, he was greeted by the cold, harsh glare of grey light coming through the caravan's curtain-less window. He sat up and grimaced, before suppressing a coughing fit. He took a moment to let his queasy, thumping head equalize to being upright, then tried to absorb his surroundings again. Somehow he'd made it back to the caravan, but he couldn't remember anything about how. He studied the crumpled clothes he still had on from the night before with a confused expression. He looked over at the other side of the bed, where Jo should have been.

It was empty and it hadn't been slept in.

Urgent thoughts began racing through his dull, aching head. He stood up and snatched open the bathroom door. It was empty too. He moved to the window and stared outside, but there was nothing to focus on, just a thick blanket of grey fog that had rolled in off the sea like a spent lover. Now he was wide-awake. Awake and full of rising anxiety.

He stumbled out through the fog, still in last night's clothes, looking like some ragged monster from an old Universal picture. He made his way awkwardly towards Crazy's caravan, calling out Jo's name, but there was no reply; his calls were just absorbed by the flat, eerie silence that lay in the thick shroud of fog that had enveloped Sweetwater. When he reached Crazy's door, he had to lean on it to steady himself, as another rush of sickness rose from the pit of his stomach to swamp his mind. He took deep breaths and banged on the door.

"Crazy," he called. "You in there? I'm coming in."

Ben opened the door and looked inside Crazy's caravan. There was nobody home, just a wall of faded photographs chronicling the crooner's yesteryears, and flyers advertising dozens of forgotten tours as a second-rate entertainer. Ben picked up one of the old pictures. It showed a much younger Crazy on stage, driving all the girls wild in some hick town watering hole.

*

Irma looked up from the bad signal on her black and white television set, where Dick Powell was about to get cold-cocked for the umpteenth time in "Farewell My Lovely". Through the office window, she could see Ben's shuffling, figure claw his way through the thick fog towards her. He opened the office door without knocking and limped up to the counter. Irma was instantly up and out of her seat to greet him with a fresh crust of bad make-up and a sickly smile.

"Have you seen Jo?" said Ben. "My girlfriend?"

Irma shook her head. Her eyes were wide with pantomime concern.

"The blonde girl I came in with...you haven't seen her at all?"

Irma slowly shook her head again. A sympathetic, but bilious smile broke out on her painted face. Ben sighed and backed out of the office looking deflated.

Had he finally done it?

Had he managed to drive her away for good this time?

He felt that burning fear in his gut again, the one that usually fired up when his bravado died down; the thought of the damage his actions might have caused, the realization that he'd probably gone too far again, that he'd inflicted too much pain and there was no salvaging their love now.

Maybe, or was her absence something else?

Was it Sweetwater?

He thought of the Black Cat and its patrons the night before. Dark memories of Ali and Dr. Harris returned to him, then darker thoughts of Henry Ho. He remembered the peephole in their hotel room and a deeper worry bled into his brain. His eyes narrowed as they tried to pierce the fog both around him and inside his head.

*

Henry Ho held the front door open with his rear and carefully backed out on to his porch. He had a tin of white paint in each hand and a paintbrush clamped between his teeth. He set the tins down and tried unsuccessfully to prize one of the lids off with his fingernails.

"Not really painting weather," said Ben. "Is it?"

Ho looked out into the fog and saw Ben approaching the hotel. He tracked Ben's limp, as he climbed the steps to his porch.

"The elements are harsh out here," said Ho. "It's got to be protected."

Ho left the paint tins and leaned against the porch railing. Ben smiled and began rolling a cigarette. He began to smoke it in silence, watching Ho carefully.

"So," Ben said eventually. "You getting ready for next season?"

"What can I say," replied Ho. "I'm an optimist."

"I don't suppose you had a pissed off lady check in here last night," said Ben. "Or if you did, I don't suppose you'd want to tell her boyfriend about it?"

"Well," said Ho. "That kind of depends on what he did to piss her off. And what he's going to do to put it right."

"Give her some flowers," said Ben. "Make up."

Ho looked Ben up and down. There was a dry expression on the hotelier's face.

"I don't see any flowers," he said.

Ben faked a smile and flicked his cigarette on to the porch.

"Where's Jo?"

"Your girlfriend didn't check-in here, Mr. Barker."

Ben rode his rising temper, trying his best to keep his cool, or at least the appearance of cool.

"So, what happened in the bar last night?" he said.

"You had a little too much to drink," said Ho. "You argued with your woman, and then, just about everyone in the bar, and eventually you passed out."

"Is that right?" said Ben.

"It was quite entertaining actually," said Ho. "Maybe we should book you to perform instead of Crazy next time."

Ben took a step closer, but Ho held his ground, showed no sign of fear.

"I know about your little peeping tom routine," said Ben. "I'm coming back here with the police. We'll let them ask you a few questions."

Ho looked unconcerned. He flashed Ben his best front-of-house grin, as he pulled a screwdriver from his pocket.

"For what it's worth," said Ho. "I'm sure your girlfriend will return when she's cooled off."

Then the grin vanished, and Ho's face turned to stone.

"Now get the fuck off my property."

Ben watched Ho return to his paint tins, kneeling down to prize the lid off one with the screwdriver.

"Sure," said Ben. "See you soon."

CHAPTER THIRTEEN

Ben made his way down Sweetwater's murky, deserted high street, now barely visible through the fog. He took a long, hurt look at the doorway of The Black Cat before approaching it. He tried the door, but it was locked, so he hammered on it and waited.

"Jo," he called. "Jo, are you in there?"

There was no response.

He tired the door again in frustration, but it wouldn't give. He backed off and circled around, wondering what to do next, but his frustrations got the better of him and he returned to pummel the door with both fists. There was still no answer from inside. After a minute, he lowered his hands to his sides, feeling flat and defeated.

The squeak of a slowly turning bicycle wheel, badly in need of oil, caught his attention. He turned around in time to see an amorphous figure on a bicycle sail past through the fog.

"Excuse me," he began. "Have you seen...?"

It was no good. The rider was already gone, dissolved into the fog. Only the sound of the squeaking wheel lingered for a few moments, growing weaker and weaker, before fading away to nothing. Ben sighed and limped off in its direction.

Ben approached Mrs. Olander's general store and tried that door too. Again, it was locked. He cupped his hands against the window and peered in through the glass at the darkened interior, but he could see no one inside. The thick, heavy pull of dread was in his belly and his chest now. He knew nothing for sure about Jo's whereabouts, but he felt in his gut that the longer he waited the less chance he would have of talking her back round. That was, if she hadn't left town already.

*

Ben walked along the coastal road, limping downhill through a thick, silent haze of fog. The town had been useless to him in his search for Jo. It seemed everyone in Sweetwater was conveniently out and there was no help to be had anywhere. He decided he needed to find Harris. He still wasn't sure what was real or imagined from his fragmented, and frankly, wild recollection of the night before, but the doctor had certainly featured heavily in the bad dreams that had followed. He would find Harris and shake the answers out of him if he had to, but first he'd need to find someone to tell him where the doctor lived.

The straining buzz of an overtaxed little moped engine climbed towards Ben through the thick fog. Desperate to interrogate somebody, anybody, he positioned himself out in the centre of the road with his arms outstretched, ready to stop the rider.

Leyton was doing no more than thirty when he emerged from the fog, but visibility was so poor that he didn't spot Ben until the last minute and had to swerve sharply to miss him. Leyton pulled the moped sharply away to one side, but Ben sidestepped back into his path to block him again. This forced Leyton to lean in even further to avoid him, forcing his moped so far over that the angle was too steep to recover from. Leyton lost control of the moped and slipped away from it as the two parted company. He rolled over and over across the gravel, as the moped crunched on to its side and slid to a halt ahead of him. Ben followed Leyton and stood over him, waiting for him to recover. The surfer groaned and struggled to his feet, his elbows and forearms skinned and raw and pitted with gravel.

"What's wrong with you, man?" he moaned.

"Tell me you didn't make a move on Jo last night," said Ben.

Leyton stared at the scraped moped lying on its side ten feet away, and suddenly forgot all about his injuries.

"Aw man, my bike" he said. "Was that fucking deliberate?"

"Where's my girlfriend?" said Ben.

Leyton frowned at him and braced up. He marched towards Ben, spoiling for a fight.

"Did you just fuck my bike up on purpose?"

The two men squared up to each other, though Ben's aggression was winding down, as Leyton began to pump his up.

"Just answer the question."

"Why you Pom-fuck..."

Leyton threw the first punch, but Ben saw it coming and pulled back, almost out of range, so that it glanced off his jaw. Leyton over-extended himself in the process and Ben quickly ducked in under the other man's outstretched arm and took advantage of the clear shot at his chin, catching Leyton with a hard uppercut. Both men then grabbed on to each other and hit the ground wrestling, rolling over and over, back and forth, each trying to dominate the other. Leyton took two fistfuls of Ben's hair and smashed his head back against the road. Ben tried to push Leyton's face away, but the surfer cracked Ben's head against the ground again, stunning him. Ben felt dazed and disoriented as he struggled against the Australian, trying to stop a third attempt. As they grappled, Ben reached down past Leyton's board shorts and found the straps securing the other man's prosthetic leg. Ben closed his eyes and moaned, as his skull thudded back against the ground again. He continued to work at the straps, as his head began to swim, and he felt himself slide towards unconsciousness. Then one of the straps on Leyton's prosthetic leg gave way in his hand.

Leyton instantly stopped fighting and looked down at Ben with surprise. Ben used the distraction to hit him with his free hand, knocking Leyton right over to the side and on to the ground. Before Leyton could recover, Ben ripped off his adversary's prosthetic leg and swung it at him.

Hard.

There was a sharp knock, as the leg caught Leyton full in the face. Ben immediately swung again without thinking, wielding the leg like a club. Leyton screamed out in pain, as two of his front teeth flew out of his mouth and across the road. Ben stood up, breathless. Leyton groveled on all fours beneath him, spitting gobs of thick, dark blood on to the gravel. Ben raised the leg, ready to strike again.

"Now," he said. "I'm going to ask you one more time. Where's my girlfriend?"

"Fucking hell," spat Leyton. "I don't know, OK. I never touched her."

"You better not be lying," said Ben.

"I'm telling you," whined Leyton. "Have a go at the Doc if you're going to have a go at anyone."

"Harris?"

Leyton laughed, then coughed and spat more blood.

"You don't remember," said Leyton. "Do you?"

Ben ignored this, tried to stay on target.

"Where's he work?" he said.

The surfer gave him a surly look, so Ben wound back the leg and prepared to swing again.

"He's got a house over the back there," said Leyton quickly. "First, no, second left turning off this road, on the way out of town."

"Thanks," said Ben.

"Can't remember," said Leyton, now chuckling to himself. "Some heavy drinker you are mate. Yeah, you're the real fuckin' deal alright."

"Mind if I borrow your bike?" said Ben.

Before the other man could reply, Ben struck him again with the prosthetic leg, swinging it like a golfer teeing off. Leyton groaned and hit the ground, out for the count. Ben threw the prosthetic leg to the side of the road and walked over to the stricken moped. He righted it and kicked over the engine. To his relief it started first time. Ben revved the moped and skidded away into the fog, disappearing in the direction Leyton had pointed out.

Ben struggled to see much of the road ahead through the continuing fog and found that he was already past the first turning before he even knew it was there, so he slowed the moped right down to a crawl and remained watchful for the next turning. A couple of minutes later it emerged from the fog, and he leaned the moped over in plenty of time to take the side road on offer. Within a few moments he sensed something looming up ahead in the fog. It was no more than a vague impression, but he slowed the moped again, just to be sure. As he idled forwards with the engine sputtering, a large structure began to take the shape of a solitary, white homestead. Ben rolled the moped to a halt and stared up at the big house's weathered facade, with its peeling white paint, cracked windows and crooked wooden fence that lay flat in several places, no doubt felled by the strong coastal winds. He left the moped and approached on foot, ascending a series of wide steps to a large, tired looking front door. He knocked and waited, but no one came. He looked around, then tried the door and found, to his surprise, it was already open. Ben hesitated, then warily stepped through into a dim, unlit hallway, complete with dusty framed paintings and faded Mackintosh print wallpaper, lined with a row of cheap looking plastic chairs set back against the wall. Bland muzak, straight out of some forgettable sixties romantic comedy, bled through from a wall mounted speaker by the doorway at the far end of the hall. Ben followed it.

"Hello?" he said.

Ben made his way down the hall and reached the door at the end that had been left slightly ajar. There was a tarnished bronze plaque on it.

It read:

Dr. Robert Harris

"Hello?" he said again.

He pushed the door open to reveal a large doctor's office, complete with writing desk, high-back leather chair, examination table and sleeping practitioner.

Harris was dressed in his white lab coat and slumped on his side across the examination table. He was out like a light. Ben waited for a moment, watching the man sleep to be certain he wasn't about to wake up, before he crept into the room. Something on the wall behind the doctor's desk caught his eye and he moved closer to examine it. It was a framed color photo of a man lying on an operating table. A cropped, faceless nurse's hands held up the patient's injured left leg for the camera. Most of the underside of the thigh was denuded of flesh, presumably removed by a large shark judging by the size and shape of the bite mark, exposing the shiny, porcelain colored bone beneath. Ben looked at another picture that hung next to it. It was the same table with the same framing, but the patient was different. This one was a cadaverous rendition of the Venus De Milo. The grey skin and total absence of both arms made Ben suspect this female patient hadn't lasted very long. He traced numerous other framed photographs of shark attack victims arranged around the surgery's walls, until he found himself coming full circle and facing Harris again. To his surprise the doctor was now awake and sitting up.

"Pretty, eh?" said Harris. "They don't work though. People don't take any notice. They still go out there."

The doctor seemed like a different person today. It was almost as if the man didn't recognize him. Ben watched him carefully.

"It looks like they keep you busy," he said.

"Not so much now, but those last couple of seasons when Sweetwater still had tourists..." Harris said, shaking his head. "...things got so bad, the government paid for me to be stationed out here permanently. It seemed like a dream gig at the time. From a research point of view anyway."

"For some reason I didn't think you were a real doctor."

Harris tapped his chest.

"Real enough."

Ben smiled, playing along.

"So, what happened after our little competition last night?"

Harris stared at him with what appeared to be genuine confusion. Ben noticed something different about Harris's eyes. Other than being blood-shot, the real difference was that they seemed much calmer and kinder than he remembered.

"In particular," he continued. "What happened to my girlfriend?"

"I'm sorry," said Harris. "What do you mean by competition?"

"Our drinking competition. In The Black Cat."

A look of shameful regret descended on Harris's features, and he turned away.

"I thought I recognized you," he said.

Harris paced away from Ben, then circled back to the examination table. He hopped up on it and began rubbing at the back of his neck. He showed Ben an embarrassed smile.

"I'm afraid you probably remember more about last night than I do," he said.

"Well," said Ben. "I remember that you were rude and aggressive. And that your hands were all over Jo. Does that help?"

Harris sighed, but didn't look surprised by the revelation.

"I'm really, really sorry. Please believe me, I don't remember anything."

Ben heard a woman's voice behind him.

"The doctor has a little problem with blackouts. Maybe I can help?"

Ben turned to see Kim, the beautiful Asian woman who was at Harris's side the night before. It turned out she really was his nurse, or at least she dressed like it.

"Blackouts?" said Ben. "You mean you're a drunk."

Kim slid between the two men, as Ben advanced on the sheepish looking doctor. Something in her dark eyes held him in check.

"Look," he said. "I don't give a flying fuck about your little nighttime games or your bad behavior. I just want to find my girlfriend."

"Easy," said Kim. "I don't like your tone."

"And I don't like being drugged and waking up to find my girlfriend gone."

"Nobody drugged you," said Kim. "You just couldn't handle your drink. You turned into a complete asshole and your girl left. That's it. Ask anybody."

"Yeah?" said Ben. "Then how come I remember you two putting moves on her?"

"In your sick little head maybe," said Kim. "Listen cowboy, you were in such a state last night, you insulted the whole bar, pissed your pants and then passed out. Anyone will tell you that."

"So you keep saying," said Ben. "I guess you won't mind if I take a look around then."

Ben marched towards a second door set in the far wall of the surgery and snatched it open.

"Don't," said Harris.

Ben flinched, as a tide of severed arms and legs spilled out of the storage room and tumbled towards him. He instinctively thrashed against the wave of limbs burying him, but it took several frantic moments to free himself. When he finally managed to scramble clear of the limbs, he looked down to see a pile of medical prosthetic arms and legs scattered across the floor. A sigh of relief escaped his lips, and he felt his breathing slow and his shoulders slump. He stood and turned to apologize to Harris, but found Kim up in his face instead.

"Get out," she said.

"I just wanted..." he began.

He stopped when Kim pulled a scalpel from the pocket of her nurse's uniform.

"Now listen," he said.

But Kim wasn't listening.

She advanced on him, slashing the scalpel across his path. The steel flashed in front of his eyes, as he raised his hands to protect himself. A thin whip of pain flared in the palm of his right hand, and he staggered backwards cradling it. He looked at Kim in disbelief and saw that she was more than willing to strike again if he pressed his luck.

"You must have a phone, or a radio here," he said, still backtracking. "At least let me use it to..."

Kim advanced on him again and raised the scalpel. Ben quickly retreated into the hallway, where the waiting room muzak still played like a long joke gone bad. Kim kept coming at him, forcing him all the way back to the door.

"Please," he began. "I just need to..."

"Get the fuck out," said Kim, quietly.

Ben stumbled out backwards through the door and quickly closed it behind him. He retreated down the front steps and looked up at the large, white, flaking house with a forlorn expression. Was his booze-soaked mind creating memories of things that hadn't happened, illusions designed to protect him from the ugly truth? The truth that he was a coward, a weak and abusive liar that had promised Jo a fresh start and then turned around and publicly spat in her face. The truth that he had drunkenly dismissed their relationship in one night, that he had discarded all that they had, all that they worked for. The truth that it was over for good this time, and that it really was all his fault.

No.

She wouldn't just disappear, he told himself. If she really was leaving him, she would want to look him in the eye first, when he was sober. She would want to make sure he fully understood what he had done, what he was losing; she would want to end it properly, for good. There must be more to it.

This last thought should have made him feel better, but it didn't. It just convinced him that despite their problems and his recent behavior, Jo's disappearance wasn't voluntary. Someone had taken her. He tried to imagine all the other possibilities for her disappearance, and how he might narrow them down to the true cause, but in his heart, he knew she had been taken. A thick, heavy, bleak feeling of helplessness began to slide over him as he felt overwhelmed at the conclusion.

CHAPTER FOURTEEN

Ben slipped out of the fog on Leyton's moped and cut the engine, letting it coast silently towards Lonesome's garage. He left it out on the roadside and walked past the sea of scrap surrounding the garage. He entered Lonesome's workshop and looked around. There was no sign of his Camper van anywhere. He heard a toilet flush behind him and turned to see Lonesome emerging from the can. The mechanic's surprise at seeing Ben standing there was obvious.

"I need to use your phone," said Ben.

"There's no phones in Sweetwater," said Lonesome. "They never bothered with lines this far out."

"Your radio then. You can't be a mechanic out here unless you've got something to talk on."

Lonesome gave him a dirty look and shuffled from one foot to another, as the wheels in his head began to turn.

"It's an emergency," said Ben.

Lonesome sighed and reluctantly nodded.

"Back here," he said.

Ben followed Lonesome into the back office. Faded nudie pictures seemed to adorn every inch of the walls and more random car parts littered the mechanic's floor and desk. Lonesome lifted a stack of Haynes manuals off a large, antiquated radio and turned it on.

"Who do you want?" he said.

"Police," said Ben. "My girlfriend's missing."

Ben stood behind Lonesome, watching him fiddle with the radio's crackling tuner. He caught sight of his own reflection in a mirror hanging on the wall. His eyes immediately focused on Jo's surfboard pendant hanging around his neck, as it caught the glare of the fluorescent strip lighting overhead. Ben stared at the pendant and thought about Jo. His mind began to lose itself in a swirl of dread and regret again. When he woke that morning to find Jo gone, he was worried she'd finally had enough and decided to leave him, but now he was scared she'd done nothing of the kind. He was scared it was this place, and one of the maniacs who lived here, that was responsible for her disappearance.

"...they can't make it out until tonight." said Lonesome.

"What?" said Ben, re-tuning into the here and now.

"The police won't be able to get out here until late tonight," said Lonesome. "Some bad road accident out west's got them all tied up."

Ben began to pace, as his mind raced through his available options.

"They said you should wait at the trailer park," said Lonesome quickly. "And that they'll meet you there when they can."

Ben nodded absently, still lost to his thoughts. He turned and limped back out across the workshop, with Lonesome sauntering after him. Ben then stopped and frowned at the mechanic.

"Where's my Camper van?"

"It's at my main scrap yard a few miles out of town," said Lonesome. "I'm looking for parts for your repair."

Lonesome gestured to the assortment of motor spares covering the workshop floor.

"This stuff's just the tip of the iceberg."

Ben's eyes lingered on Lonesome's features, searching the man's face for a tell of some kind. But there were no obvious signs, even though Ben knew he was lying.

"Have you seen Crazy?" said Ben.

"Crazy? Nah., I suppose you could try the golf course."

"The golf course?"

Ben's look of confusion slowly turned to realization, as he remembered the junkyard at the back of Crazy's beach shack.

"Oh yeah," he said. "The golf course."

*

The headlight on Leyton's scooter cut through a faint shroud of fog still covering the beach. The mist was beginning to thin rapidly now, especially since the wind had picked up to help it on its way. Ben slowed the scooter and parked it out on the beach road. As he waded through the dissipating fog towards "Crazy's Golf", strange, huge shapes begin to form ahead of him, like prehistoric beasts emerging from some forgotten land. These shapes slowly revealed themselves as post-apocalyptic towers of rusting scrap metal and elaborate driftwood constructions; salt-bitten landmarks that mapped out Sweetwater's own novelty golf course.

Ben saw Crazy slumped down against a large, disused water tank that lay on its side with arced sections cut out to allow golfers to play through its innards and back out again. Crazy sat beneath the edifice like a sacrifice at the altar of some gigantic, rusting deity. He looked up at Ben with large, melancholy eyes as he approached. He then deliberately looked away again and took a swig from a bottle of whiskey.

"Hard at it?" said Ben.

Crazy shrugged with the heavy, exaggerated movements of a drunk.

"It's my day off," he said.

Ben sat down next to him. Crazy handed him the bottle. Ben held it in his hands without taking a hit. He just brooded over the golden liquid inside.

"Why the hell did you ever build this monstrosity?" he said.

"I made the best of what was to hand," said Crazy. "That's all anyone can do around here."

"I actually kind of like it. It doesn't pretend to be something it's not."

"Everyone's a critic."

Ben took a last look at the booze and handed it back to Crazy.

"Where is she?" he said.

Crazy stared dead ahead, but there was nothing to see, only more fog. He lifted the bottle again, but Ben rested his hand on it and stopped him. Ben moved closer and looked the older man in the eye.

"Where is she?"

"You know, I've been in Sweetwater nearly twenty years now. And I'm still an outsider."

Ben let go of the bottle. He slipped his hand into his pocket, retrieved his tobacco and began to roll a cigarette. He lit it without taking his eyes off Crazy.

"Sometimes, you just want to go home," said the old man. "You know? You need to go home. But then you realize...you realize you don't know where that is anymore."

"You tried to warn me yesterday, didn't you?"

Crazy took a deep breath and looked at the bottle again. Ben could see it was an effort for the older man to keep it from his lips.

"I like you Ben, I really do. Forget about Sweetwater and go, get out of here any way you can."

"It's too late for that now."

"Forget her. Just go."

Ben grabbed two fistfuls of Crazy's dusty tuxedo and hauled him to his feet, shaking him.

"Tell me where she is," he snapped. "Please Joe."

Crazy looked at him. There was a somber expression on his craggy face.

"You know Irma?" he said. "She was always talking. I mean she was a regular chatterbox. One day, there was this family, with a couple of cute kids. They stayed at the van park. Now Irma never had any children of her own. So it wasn't a surprise to any of us when she took a liking to those kids."

Crazy looked at the ground for a moment, at the booze, and then finally faced Ben again.

"So, of course, her conscience started up, and I guess it began gnawing away at her. She didn't think it was right, what they were planning. And so she spoke up. She warned those folks. She told them to get away. Do you know what the others did to her when they found out?"

Crazy put his finger to his lips and whispered the slightest shush.

"They cut her tongue out."

Ben slammed Crazy back against the rusting metal tank, but then quickly turned away from the old man before he did something he'd regret.

Crazy lifted the bottle and took another hit.

"I don't know why they still go to all that trouble. So much blood. And it never works. It never changes anything."

Ben circled back and grabbed Crazy again, stared into his eyes.

"What never works?" he said.

The older man shrugged and tried to lift the bottle again. Ben smacked it out of his hand and it exploded on the ground. Crazy watched the escaping booze soak into the earth with what seemed like a profound sense of loss. The old singer was coming apart at the seams.

"Crazy," said Ben. "Joe...where do I find her?"

Crazy looked at him, suddenly sober again.

"They're going to kill me for talking to you."

Crazy picked Ben's cigarette up off the ground and pulled on it. He closed his eyes, relishing the taste; the condemned man's last request. He sighed.

"She'll be at the cannery, or the hotel."

"Thank you."

Crazy nodded and stared out into the fog. No problem, he thought. I was through with this life anyway. Maybe I'll make a better go of things next time around.

Something flashed up ahead of them in the fog. Ben stared along the beach and spotted what looked like the headlights of a stationary vehicle. Anger flashed in his eyes. He left Crazy and began limping towards the glow. Crazy staggered back over to the tank and began urinating against it. He began muttering the song "Viva Las Vegas" to himself.

Ben strained to see, as he waded through the dissolving fog across the beach. The vehicle ahead of him slowly began to take shape. Soon, enough of it was revealed for Ben to recognize it. It was the freezer van that ran him off the road out of town, stranding him in Sweetwater.

"Motherfucker..." he whispered to himself.

Ben picked up the pace, dragging his prosthetic leg as he limped towards the van.

"Crazy!" he shouted back. "Crazy, it's them!"

He heard the van's engine being gunned and its tires squeal as it accelerated away. The Van left the road and swerved at Ben, forcing him to dive into the sand. The van sped past, narrowly missing him, then mounted the road again, heading towards "Crazy's Golf". Ben picked himself up in time to see it screech to a halt there.

"Crazy," he said.

Ben began to rush back towards the golf course. He could make out the van's red taillights piercing the fog and hear its engine running. As he drew nearer, he could make out the figure of a man drag something towards the van's rear. He heard its tail shutter lift open and then slam shut. He was close now, close enough to see the figure climb back into the front of the van. He could make out a cartoon jumping fish painted on the side of the van, next to the words "Always Fresh – Olander's" written beneath.

The freezer van's tires squealed again, burning rubber as it pulled away sharply, its rear lights quickly retreating into the mist. Ben stumbled back to the crazy golf course. He was out of breath, filled with panic and unable to see the old man anywhere.

Crazy!" he shouted. "Crazy!"

Ben jumped on Leyton's moped and started it up. He aimed it in the direction of the disappearing van and raced off in pursuit. The shroud of fog was still thicker away from the beach and Ben could barely see anything ahead. He snatched small glimpses of gravel road and little else, but he could hear the van's engine up ahead, so he pushed the moped harder and harder. He climbed the coastal road in the opposite direction of town, but quickly became disoriented after that. There was no sign of the van's tail lights, and every now and then he had to turn sharply to hold the road, as it twisted and snaked to greater heights.

After a few moments, a surreal sense of isolation and inertia closed in around Ben. With no horizon, and surrounded by fog, he seemed to be speeding along in his own serene bubble. There was a comfort in the sensation and the drone of the moped's engine almost lulled him into a trance-like state. The spell was broken when he saw headlights flash on in the distance ahead and then sweep around towards him. Suddenly the van's engine was bearing down on him.

Ben yanked the moped to one side and it glanced off the edge of the van's bull bars. The moped skidded away along the road, as Ben was separated from it, bouncing through the air. He hit the gravel and rolled across it, ripping up his clothes and skin. Then there was nothing beneath him. He instinctively reached out, panicking, and gripped on to bare rock, as he felt his legs swing out and dangle into thin air. He yelled and opened his eyes to find himself hugging a cliff edge. His feet scrabbled against the rock's surface and managed to find purchase. A series of clanging sounds rang out far below, as falling gravel showered down and ricocheted off something metallic at the foot of the cliff. Ben clung on tightly to the rock face and looked up to see the van's headlights illuminating the jagged cliff edge he had skidded off. The headlights then retreated and swept away, as the van reversed and turned back down the road.

Ben strained and pulled himself back up on to the cliff edge. He peered back over the side and down into the abyss below. A large, swirling patch of fog was drifting away, as the sea breeze slowly chased it from the cliffs. Ben stared down through the window opening in the fog as it gradually expanded. It slowly revealed a long, steep drop down into a narrow ravine, ending in a rocky overlap of spurs near the ground. There, at the bottom of the ravine, Ben saw vehicle upon dead vehicle, all smashed and impacted against the rocks. It was a twisted heap of tangled metal. More than a dozen abandoned cars and Camper vans covered the floor of the ravine. Ben stared down at the metal graveyard in horror. The stripped and crumpled skeleton of his own Camper van lay on the top of the pile.

Ben grimaced with pain from his scraped and bruised joints, as he staggered back over to Leyton's moped. He righted it and tried the engine, but it failed to turn over. He cursed himself and tried it again.

Nothing.

Ben stared out into the fog in the direction he imagined the cannery to be, as he tried the engine again and again. His fear for Jo was all consuming now. He tried not to think about what might be happening to her or Crazy at that very moment.

CHAPTER FIFTEEN

Crazy stirred. His eyes blinked open and he moaned, as a sharp ache awoke too and throbbed in his head and arms. He scanned his new surroundings and tried to orientate himself. He was suspended from a rope just above the deck of The Lady Ann, moored at the end of Olander's jetty. He tried to move as he slowly twisted on the rope, but couldn't. His arms had been lashed tightly to his sides, wound around his midsection by the same rope that held him. He looked up and saw it was pulled taut and fed through the boat's winch arm.

Most of the fog had been carried away by the wind, but drifting trails still lingered in wisps here and there over the water. Crazy listened and heard a faint, regular splashing sound coming from the boat's stern. He twisted to look in that direction and saw a figure hunched over the stern's rail, shoveling fish guts from a bucket and dumping them over the side into the water.

The splashing stopped and the hunched figure rose and slowly approached him. It was Olander. The fisherman looked Crazy up and down with a flat stare, but said nothing. Crazy heard more footsteps approaching and turned to see Ali there too. The Maori joined Olander and the two men stood in front of Crazy. Ali tutted at Crazy and shook his head. His eyes were bright, alert and taunting. He was clearly savoring Crazy's obvious fear. Olander, on the other hand, seemed more workman-like than his accomplice, as if the real gravity of the situation eluded him. He smoked a cigarette, and shuffled about, apparently eager to crack on with the job at hand.

Crazy dropped his head forlornly and stared down at the deck for a moment. He didn't know exactly what was coming next, but he had a good idea. Screw them, he thought. He'd toed the line with these maniacs for long enough. He didn't believe what they believed, and he never had. He knew he'd been a joke to this town ever since he arrived, even though most of them had never been anywhere, never tasted the world. He on the other hand, had always played his hand, always tried his luck. That hand had seen him travel all over the globe and experience many different lands, people and cultures before Sweetwater. And he was proud of that sense of adventure and the chapters it had given him. If this was it, if this was the end, he would go out with his head held high. He straightened up and looked Ali in the eye.

"I won't scream," he said.

Ali moved closer and drew his hunting blade from his belt. Olander stepped forwards too and took hold of Crazy's head. The old man struggled in vain, as the sturdy fisherman overpowered him and prized his jaws open.

"I know," said Ali.

Ali reached into Crazy's mouth and tugged his tongue out straight. He then angled the knife towards Crazy's mouth and sawed through the tongue, severing it in just three strokes. Crazy shook violently, as blood erupted from his mouth. Ali stepped back with a sadistic grin on his face. He casually tossed the singer's tongue overboard. Seconds later, there was a splash, as something broke the water's surface to claim it.

Olander turned to the winch handle and began to crank it furiously. Crazy was lifted higher into the air, as blood continued to pour from his mouth, splattering down over the deck in wild Pollackesque trails.

Ali looked on smugly, as the winch arm swung Crazy out over the side of the boat and dangled him above the red, recently chummed waters. More blood dripped down from Crazy's butchered tongue and into the water. Something large and dark surfaced and splashed, before quickly disappearing. Crazy began to thrash and kick his legs and cry out, but only stunted moaning sounds managed to escape his mouth.

Ali nodded to Olander and the fisherman began to reverse the winch crank. Crazy wrestled frantically against his bonds, as he was slowly lowered towards the sea. His eyes grew wide with terror, as his lower half submerged into the rising, reddening water until it lapped against his chest. Dark shapes moved beneath him, as his eyes tried to trace the numerous unseen predators rising up from the depths. More splashes broke the surface around him, making him flinch. He shook his head and screwed his eyes shut, waiting for the inevitable to happen.

Ali smiled and nodded at Olander, and the fisherman went to work on the winch again. Crazy's eyes snapped open, as he felt himself being lifted out of the water. He tightened, as something large bumped against his dripping feet, dangling just inches above the surface. He began muttering a prayer over and over, the words of which were indistinguishable coming from his severed tongue. He now hovered a foot above the water, his whole-body shivering with uncontrollable fear.

Ali signaled to Olander to wind the winch down again. The fisherman let out a loud sigh and reluctantly began lowering Crazy again. Crazy watched the approaching water, as he was slowly dipped back into a dark sea brimming with writhing, half-glimpsed shapes. This time Olander stayed on the winch until Crazy was dunked all the way up to his chin. Crazy scanned the surface of the water and saw something large gliding towards him. He closed his eyes again and braced himself.

Nothing.

Crazy's face was still frozen in a grimace of dread when he slowly opened his fearful eyes to look. Just as he did, the head of an enormous great white burst from the water only inches away from his face. Its massive jaws extended out from its jutting mouth to tear into Crazy's shoulder. Crazy let out a silent scream and threw his head back in terror, as the great white scissored off his entire right arm and slipped beneath the waves with it.

Ali hurriedly motioned for Olander to winch their victim back up again, his eyes now wide and excited with the thrill of torture. Crazy's sodden, twitching body hung limp as it was hauled out of the water. He groaned and rolled his delirious eyes, suspended over the surface, with arterial red still jetting from the remains of his shoulder.

Ali turned to Olander and barked orders.

"Slowly, slowly," he shouted.

Olander stopped winching and growled something under his breath. He gave the other man an angry look and then slapped the break off the winch.

Crazy was instantly dumped beneath the waves.

Ali glared at Olander and marched towards him. The fisherman turned to face him head on. Neither man noticed Crazy's rope pull taught, as another unseen shark took the bait.

A distant buzzing sound roused Ali and Olander from their confrontation. They both looked up to see the lights of Leyton's scooter, as it picked its way down the cliff road towards the cannery. Ali shot Olander an urgent glance and began rushing back along the jetty. Olander turned and looked back into the churning red water, as Crazy was devoured somewhere in the depths below.

*

Ben cut the moped's engine and coasted downhill towards the abandoned cannery. He saw Olander's white freezer van parked beside the cannery's loading bay and felt his stomach turn and tighten. He broke behind it and left the moped leaning against the bay. He carefully crept up to a side window and tried to peer inside the building, but the windows were so filthy they were nearly opaque and impossible to see through. Ben crept back along the corrugated metal siding and lingered at the corner of the open loading bay, where a corona of fluorescent light was spilling out. He took a deep breath and edged inside.

Ben moved slowly, his eyes constantly searching the cannery's grimy, mechanical interior. The stench of rotten fish was overpowering inside, and he had to concentrate hard to stop himself from retching.

Production here was obviously a thing of the past. Canning machinery lay rusting in the centre of the hanger, traversed by a snaking conveyer belt. Tired looking walk-in freezers, some left open, lined the rear of the building, and large loops of redundant chains and winches hung from the ceiling like limp tendrils.

Ben crept past towering stacks of empty wooden pallets and peered around the corner of the wall they formed. He saw a series of fish cleaning stations set in a row. A figure worked at one of them with his back to Ben, his arms elbow-deep in a huge metal sink. Next to the man there were several vats of boiling water bubbling away on gas burners. The man turned and reached into one of the vats with a long set of iron tongues. Ben could now see that it was Ali, the Maori bartender from the Black Cat. Ali fished a set of freshly bleached shark jaws out of the vat and examined them. Ben noticed a machete blade buried into a wooden chopping block on the counter next to Ali and swallowed. He slowly began to sneak up on Ali, his eyes constantly switching between the Maori's broad back and the machete he was aiming for. Ben limped closer and closer to the machete, flinching with every clumsy step his prosthetic leg took, fully expecting the Maori to hear and turn on him at any moment. As those thoughts filled his head, Ben's trainer stepped into a large pool of blackened fish blood that had slowly been draining from one of the cleaning stations. His prosthetic leg immediately slid forwards uncontrollably, making him wobble. He struggled to keep his balance, before righting himself again, but when he looked up, he saw Ali watching him with a predatory grin.

The two men stared at each other for what seemed like a long time. When Ben finally looked away at the machete buried midway between them, Ali turned to stare at it too. Ben was scared. This man was much bigger, stronger and certainly faster than him. If he was a little closer, maybe he might be able to reach the machete first, but as things were, he doubted his chances.

Ali pulled a sliver cross on a chain from beneath the neckline of his tee-shirt and began toying with it. It was Ben's cross, the one he'd given to Jo. The implication was clear. Ben stared at the cross and seethed inside. Ali's eyes remained on Ben the whole time, as his mouth began to spread into a wide grin, offering up an obvious challenge.

Ben's fear was pushed aside by the swell of anger inside his head. His muscles tightened and braced, and then he launched himself towards the machete as fast as he could.

Ali moved too.

Faster.

When Ben reached the machete, Ali was already there waiting for him. The big Maori left the machete where it was and grabbed Ben by the throat instead, easily spinning him around and smashing him back into the wooden counter. Ben moaned as Ali throttled him with one huge hand and simultaneously backhanded with the other. Three more of these blows followed, quickly belting Ben senseless. Then, with one hand still closed tightly around Ben's throat, Ali casually drove him back towards one of the large steel vats of boiling water.

Ben flinched as his face was pushed down towards the scalding water and he felt the rising heat sear his skin. He grabbed on to the edge of the fish gutting station, trying to resist, but Ali was far too strong for him. Ben's straining features were slowly forced closer and closer to the bubbling water. He spotted the hunting knife sheathed in Ali's belt and immediately reached for it, while still pushing back against the man's chokehold. His fingers quickly closed around the knife's handle, and he slipped it free, turning it and plunging it straight back into Ali's belly in one fluid movement.

Ali growled and staggered backwards, releasing Ben as he did so. He stared down at the knife stuck in his gut and then back up again at Ben with a look of genuine surprise, which quickly turned to fury. Ali left the knife where it was and lunged forwards at Ben, who was too exhausted to avoid the attack. Ali's hands closed around Ben's throat, and he proceeded to choke him again. Ben reached for the knife handle again and twisted it deep into Ali's belly. Ali howled and immediately released his grip. Ben took his chance and pushed him backwards, steering his head down into the vat of boiling water to dunk it.

Ali screamed and writhed on contact with the water as if he was being electrocuted. His hands flailed and found purchase on the counter, and he pulled his head clear of the vat.

But it was too late.

When the Maori turned to face Ben, his steaming face was red raw and covered in blisters.

Ali shook with pain and anger and then screamed at Ben.

Ben backed away, as Ali pulled the knife from his gut and advanced on him. His angry, boiled features distorted further into a furious snarl as he closed in. Ben turned and limped away as fast as he could across the factory floor. He ducked under the conveyor belt and squeezed between the production machinery, desperately trying to put some distance between himself and the Maori maniac. He heard Ali howl in pain and rage as if performing a demented haka, some way off behind him; but not far enough. Ben rushed blindly through the maze of redundant machinery, turning this way, then that, until he found himself spat out into a dead end. Ahead of him was a wall with just three closed metal doors to large walk-in freezers. He immediately started to backtrack, but Ali let out another frenzied howl behind him, this time much closer.

Ben hesitated, then made for the middle freezer and snatched the large door open. He ran straight in and found himself enveloped in an icy blast of mist. A second later it began to clear, and he found himself lunging towards a gigantic set of protruding shark jaws. He let out a startled yelp and found himself nose to nose with a huge great white shark. He instantly scrambled backwards away from the open jaws, slipping and sliding on the icy floor until he managed to reach the wall of the freezer and steady himself.

Ben moved to the side and stared down the length of the shark in awe. Only the front half of the frozen shark remained, suspended from the ceiling by a row of hooks and heavy chains. The rest of the fish had presumably been butchered and consumed, leaving a strange, abstract half-monster languishing in the freezer like an ichthyological exhibit.

Ali let out another howl outside.

Ben quickly dragged the freezer door shut and wobbled across the ice to flatten himself against the frost-covered wall. He leaned back and sighed, trying to slow his rapid breathing.

*

Ali stared at the three freezers ahead, his chest quickly rising and falling, his blood pumping through his ears. He then turned and rushed towards the left freezer and snatched the door open. A blast of cold, misty air escaped, engulfing him as he stepped inside. The mist cleared within seconds and Ali checked the freezer's interior. The cross section of another enormous great white faced him. The length-ways half of this bisected fish ran nose to tail, hung before him from the frosted ceiling like some grotesque installation.

Ali turned and ran straight to the second, middle freezer. He hauled this door open too and stepped inside, only to be greeted by another icy blast of mist. He waved the mist away, as a hazy figure began to take shape next to him. Ben reached out and grabbed Ali's arm and quickly spun him around, sliding the Maori over the ice. He thrust Ali's head towards the dead shark's open jaws and watched it disappear deep inside the fish's mouth. Ali felt razor-sharp teeth graze against the back of his neck, as his feet kicked and slipped on the icy floor of the freezer, unable to find a grip. Ali hung there for a moment like a headless Cossack, his arms flailing about blindly, as his feet kicked out this way, then that, struggling against gravity and the ice. Finally, both feet slipped from beneath him at the same time and his full weight sank against the shark's serrated teeth. Ben saw the head come clean off, as Ali's decapitated body flopped down against the ice like a puppet with its strings cut. Ali's boiled and severed head stared out at Ben in perpetual surprise from the frozen shark's mouth.

Ben emerged from the freezer in a daze, holding on to the door with both hands to remain upright. He lurched out, unsteady on his feet, then immediately doubled up and puked on to the factory floor. He stayed hunched over for a few moments, coughing up strings of phlegm and bile, trying to expel the nauseous image of what he'd just seen; what he'd just done. He then sucked in a deep breath and slowly raised his head, only to see Olander's blunt face waiting there to greet him. Ben started to speak, but Olander swung a fish club at his head and connected with a sharp crack.

Ben immediately fell back into a sea of blackness.

CHAPTER SIXTEEN

The faint sound of the sea reached Ben's ears and tried to rouse him from his sleep. He heard the call of waves bursting over rocks in the distance and slowly opened his eyes. He fought to focus on the blurred scene through a window before him. A framed view from the cliffs looking out to sea over the Great Bight gradually took shape. His view of the ocean was clear now, as was the sky, the last of the fog having burned away long ago. The sun was low in the sky, threatening to dip below the horizon and submerge itself in the waters beyond. Ben closed his eyes and groaned. The back of his skull was already ballooning with a thick, dull, queasy ache where Olander had clubbed him. He closed his eyes and tried to swallow his rising nausea. When he opened his eyes again, he looked away from the window and saw dozens of candles slowly slide into focus around him. He slowly shook his head in confusion and tried to stand. He lurched and felt more nausea churn in his stomach and head, but he finally made it to his feet.

He looked around and gradually recognized the bookshelves, papers and artifacts surrounding him. He was in Henry Ho's study. An area against the back wall had been cleared of Ho's paperwork and clutter, and a figure in red was kneeling there with his back to Ben.

It was Henry Ho.

Ho flicked his lighter repeatedly without success. Eventually it caught and he used the flame to light two lint cloth wound torches held in wall-mounted brackets. Ho slowly rose and turned to face him. He was bare chested, but wore a red ceremonial cloak over his shoulders. It looked to Ben like it had been fashioned from old curtains. A large shark tooth pendant hung around Ho's neck. Ben thought he looked little like a dumpy drag queen at a carnival in his ceremonial garb, but the image didn't make him smile.

Ho looked up at him and walked over to one of the bookshelves. He picked up a glass of whiskey and handed it to Ben, who just stared at it.

"Take it," said Ho. "You're going to need it."

The hotelier then turned and shouted to his unseen wife, without any hint of reverence.

"Honey!" He called. "Fetch me my headdress, would you?"

Ben looked at Ho coldly and placed the glass of whiskey down on the floor with no intention of drinking it.

"Where is she?" he said.

Ho moved away from a makeshift altar by the wall. Dozens more lit candles sat on a small plinth there covered by more red material. In the centre lay a large set of bleached tiger shark jaws.

Ho stared at Ben thoughtfully and slowly circled him.

"Sweetwater is being eaten alive," he said. "It's at odds with nature. It's a settlement made in a place where man was never supposed to live. If we're to survive here, we have to strive for harmony with the elements, with the sea. We have to respect nature's rules."

"Where's Jo?" said Ben.

"It's about sharing their waters, without conflict."

"I said, where is she?"

Ho sighed wearily and strolled towards the shelving near the open door at the front of his study. He shouted out through the doorway.

"Don't worry Hon, I'll get it."

Ho stretched up to the top of the adjacent bookshelf and felt about with his fingers. He then smiled and retrieved a slim, ornate golden headband. He ran it through his fingers, wiping the dust off it, then carefully positioned it on his head.

"If you don't show me Jo," said Ben. "I'm going to beat you to death with my bare hands."

"Sure..." said Ho.

Ho had his back to Ben. He was taking something else off the bookcase and tucking it under his arm. When he turned around to face Ben, the wooden handled shark tooth claw was visible in its glass display case.

"...but first, you've got to do something for me."

Ben stared at the claw and then followed Ho's eyes up to the painting above the altar. It was the dramatic image of the Hawaiian brave battling in vain against a ferocious tiger shark.

A sickly, weakening feeling slid over Ben, making him fold and lean back against the wall for support.

This, this is what they wanted.

"You're insane," said Ben quietly.

"You people are always surprised," shrugged Ho. "I don't get that. Personally, I'd have seen it coming."

"Why me?" said Ben. "What have I done?"

"Nothing," replied Ho. "It's a huge honor. All our fates rest with you today, Ben."

"No way."

"You'll do it. You'll do it because you love her."

Ben rushed him. He hit Ho in the chest and drove him backwards into the bookshelves behind him, smashing the claw's display case against the floor in the process. Ben got two good shots in, before Angie Ho appeared behind him and held him fast.

Henry Ho picked himself up, rubbing his aching jaw. He lifted up the claw, cutting his finger on a shard of smashed glass from the broken case. Ben struggled against Angie Ho, but she was every bit as strong as she looked.

"Bring him closer," said Ho.

Angie Ho pushed Ben forwards; his arms forced outwards by her headlock. Ho took hold of Ben's right hand and pressed the palm against the teeth of the shark jaws arranged on the altar. Ben struggled as blood welled up in the palm of his hand. Ho smeared his fingers with the blood and used it to paint a red cross on Ben's forehead. Ho then turned away and pulled back a thick rug in the centre of the study to reveal a heavy trapdoor set into the floorboards. He lifted a large iron ring protruding there and heaved, raising the trapdoor. A rush of dank air tainted with salty sea spray rushed up to greet them from the hollow blackness below.

Henry Ho walked back to the altar and took one of the large, glowing kindling torches from the wall behind it. He turned to look at Ben, still subdued by Angie's Ho's meaty arms.

"Are we calm now?" he said.

Ben nodded. Henry Ho gave his wife a look and she unlocked her arms from around Ben's neck. The flaming torch in Ho's hand flared in a draught rising from the tunnel below, as he approached the open trap door again. Ben could just make out the first few stone steps plunging down into blackness beneath the hotel.

"No one's going to make you," said Ho. "It doesn't work like that. You've got to be willing, otherwise the ceremony's nowhere near as powerful."

Ho began to descend, the torch illuminating the way. Ben could see that the passageway below had been carved from the bare rock the hotel stood on. He wondered how old it was and how many others had been marched down into the darkness before him. He looked back at Angie Ho with uncertainty. She replied by pushing him forwards through the trap door and they followed Ho down into the blackness.

CHAPTER SEVENTEEN

Henry Ho led the way as they wound down through the subterranean rock passageway. The chiseled steps eventually gave way to just a roughly inclined tunnel, as if a lower, older passage existed long before it was extended to reach the hotel above it. As they sank deeper into the side of the cliff, the sloping, dank passage became wetter. Water bled from the porous rock and ran down the walls and dripped on to them from the ceiling above. The wind howled up through the tunnel to greet them, making the flames on Henry Ho's torch flutter and dance. And all the time the sound of the sea swell lingered in the distance below them.

*

Red water slapped against the side of the motorboat's hull, as Olander looked up from his chumming duties. He watched the red sun on the horizon slowly begin to set. He then turned and looked at the light gradually retreating from the shadows over Sweetwater's cliffs. Ho's Palace was now just a dark, reddening shape on the cliff tops against the approaching dusk.

Olander dug his trowel deep into a large plastic tub and shoveled the bloody contents over the side. He then opened up the throttle and steered the motorboat back towards the jagged cliffs beneath the hotel.

*

Ben followed Henry Ho through the underground passageway as it leveled off and opened out into a huge, round cave beneath the cliffs. The sea had found its way in here too through the cave's mouth and deep black water filled the centre, forming a foreboding, dark underground pool. Ho moved carefully along the edge of the water on a wide ledge of rock that surrounded the pool, lighting more torches suspended in iron brackets fixed to the cave walls. Ben and Angie Ho lingered near the passageway's entrance, as Henry Ho backtracked to the other side of the pool, lighting the remaining torches - more than two dozen in all. The fires gradually illuminated the cavern, and added a ceremonial, almost medieval air to the proceedings.

Ben looked out to sea through the cave's mouth. A small motorboat with a lone figure aboard was slowly chugging towards the cave through calm seas and failing light. Ho lit the last torch and placed his own into an empty wall bracket next to the tunnel's entrance. He returned to stand next to Ben, looking smug and pious in his ceremonial headdress.

Ben's eyes fixed on the ceiling at the centre of the now fully lit cave. Jo was there, suspended above the pool by a rope, which fed back along the roof of the cave to a pulley system on the far side of the ledge. Jo was tightly bound and gagged. Even at hundred feet in this poor light, Ben could clearly make out her wide, terrified eyes pleading to him.

Ben fought to control his emotions. He was flushed with relief and hope at seeing Jo alive, but the feeling was tempered by his growing fear for both of them after Ho's speech. He knew what Ho wanted from him in return for Jo's life, and as insane as it sounded, he knew the man was deadly serious. He began to feel sick again. The nausea from his concussion mixed with the thick dread in the pit of his stomach and rose up inside him like black bile. He moaned quietly and leaned back, grabbing at the rock wall to steady himself, as the fear and anxiety turned his stomach. He took a moment to let the nausea subside, and then tried to compose himself. He had to do something now, before the boat was here, before there were too many of them to fight.

He pushed himself off the wall and rushed Henry Ho again. But he was still unsteady on his feet and Angie Ho stepped in to block the attack. She caught Ben and twisted him around, restraining him again with ease.

Henry Ho shook his head, faintly amused.

"You need to stop fighting this and focus on what lies ahead." he said. "I told you before, it's not a sacrifice. It's a duel."

Ho moved closer and looked at him earnestly.

"It can be done."

Ben stopped wrestling against Angie Ho and began to listen.

"How much do you love her?" asked Henry Ho.

Ben stared across the water at Jo. Her eyes were on him again, still terrified, still pleading. He began to wonder if he could bring himself to do it.

Something caught Ben's eye and he turned to see members of the townsfolk solemnly filing out of the passageway he'd taken. They spread out left and right along the water's edge to slowly fill the cave, until more than forty spectators lined the arc around the submerged gladiatorial arena. He saw Leyton, Harris, Kim, Lonesome, Irma, even old Mrs. Olander; everyone he'd met so far in Sweetwater was present, with the exception of Crazy and Olander. He saw that they now all wore shark tooth pendants around their necks similar to Ho's. They watched him, their faces deadly serious and tight with anticipation. He looked away from the parade of cold stares and focused on Jo instead.

"This is the old way," said Ho. "It's the natural order of things."

Ben said nothing, yet his eyes strained to try and communicate everything he felt to the woman he loved. He wanted her to know how much he loved her, that he would do anything for her, and that he would somehow save her from this.

"Your expression of courage will appease the sea. It will bring back life and prosperity to this dead town..."

Henry Ho looked at Ben, then bowed to him.

"...and we will forever honor you."

Ben heard the chug of a motorboat echo around the cave walls as it approached the arena. He turned to watch it in a queasy daze. Olander slowly guided the motorboat through the mouth of the cave, still lazily chumming the water. He weaved in and around the pool, leaving a slick, winding trail of red behind him.

Ben's eyes widened in horror, as he caught a glimpse of his intended adversary. A dorsal fin breached and cut through the surface of the water some fifty feet behind Olander's boat. The tiger shark's tail snaked and then made a little whip-like movement, as it glided in silently through the mouth of the cave and then submerged into the blackness.

Ben looked around at the line of expectant faces, all lit by the wavering light of the torch flames. They were entranced. He saw two figures move to the mouth of the cave and pull on ropes latched there. Seconds later a weighted fishing net dropped down across the entrance, trapping the shark in the pool.

Ben's gaze returned to the water, as the fin broke the surface again and started to grimly circle the black pool.

Olander's boat slowly pulled alongside Ben. Henry Ho held out the shark tooth claw for him to take.

The two men stared at each other.

Ho's features were cold and expressionless.

"We need calm waters," he said.

"You're insane," said Ben, quietly.

"It's you or her," said Ho. "At least you have a chance. She would have none."

Tears began to well up in Ben's eyes as he looked at Jo again.

Henry Ho nodded to another member of the town and the man leaned back on the pulley and let out a little slack on the rope threading back from Jo.

Jo's body jerked and she let out a muffled scream, as she dropped several feet from the cave's roof. The line snapped taught again and she dangled helplessly above the black water. She stared down in horror as the dorsal fin cruised beneath her.

"Well?" said Ho.

Ben was hypnotized. He felt as though he was walking through a dream. He'd felt a strange dislocation from reality ever since they'd arrived in Sweetwater, but this was too much for his mind to take. He couldn't fight it any longer. There was no other way out. He took the claw without a word and walked to the water's edge. He felt dozens of eyes burn into him as he climbed into the motorboat in a daze. Henry Ho followed him, and they sat together, as the boat motored out towards the centre of the pool.

Ben saw a cruel, dumb expression on Olander's features that reminded him of blank faced children fascinated with hurting animals. By contrast, Henry Ho had a look of overwhelming pride and majesty. He really believed this shit. Ben noticed the tiger's dorsal fin keeping pace with the boat. He tried to block it out and turned to concentrate on the woman he loved, as she slowly returned to him in the saltwater dungeon. As they drew near, Ben saw the terror in Jo's eyes abate for a moment, as the realization of what he was about to do dawned on her. Then she became desperately animated, shaking her head at him, writhing against the rope, her eyes imploring him not to do it.

He could only stare back with love and resignation.

He loved her.

He had no choice.

Olander cut the engine and let the boat drift to a halt in the centre of the pool, bobbing there on the water like bait. The dorsal fin rose again to cut a wake through the surface and approach the boat. It silently cruised towards them, then veered away at the last minute and broke into a tight circle around the boat. Ben could feel the weight of the townsfolk's stares on him, but he refused to look at them. He stared up at Jo one more time. His eyes wanted to say it all; what she meant to him, how sorry he was for everything, how she had saved him, and how it was only now that he really knew all of this; but in the end, that desperate desire to tell her everything was all they could communicate.

Ben drew the claw's tooth around the denim covering his leg and sliced it away to reveal the plastic prosthetic beneath. He then cut through the straps and let the imitation leg fall away. At that moment he felt a sensation of lightness; a freedom from the enormous weight of fear and guilt he had learned to carry, freedom from the past, freedom from his old self.

His last look at Ho was almost a grateful one. Unmoved, Henry Ho just nodded curtly, confirming it was time. Ben peered over the side at the black waters lapping against the boat and gripped the woodwork. The dorsal fin was nowhere to be seen now. Ben took a deep breath, closed his eyes and slid down into the water.

CHAPTER EIGHTEEN

Ben swam out into the centre of the pool, away from the motorboat, clutching the tooth-claw's handle as tightly as he could. He was still unable to see the shark, so he began to slowly rotate, treading water, bracing himself for the inevitable attack. He remembered what Ho had said, about diving beneath the shark and opening up its belly on the first pass. A one-shot deal.

Jo saw it first.

The dorsal fin surfaced forty feet away from Ben to his rear. Her muffled screams weren't enough to alert him though, as the fin closed in. She began to twist and thrash on the rope like a fish caught on a line. Ben finally looked up and saw her frantic expression, her terrified eyes focused on something behind him. He turned and caught sight of the fin disappearing, as the shark began to dive beneath the water.

Ben calmly stared straight ahead with dead eyes. He took a deep breath and sank beneath the surface. Once under the water, he opened his eyes again to see a large black shape gliding towards him. It seemed to hang in the water just above him, its silhouette illuminated by the line of flaming torches around the pool. The tiger cruised straight towards him, its motives clear. Ben used his arms to push himself lower and lower as it approached. When the charge came, he dived as low as he could, and reached up towards the advancing tiger's belly with the outstretched claw. He thrust the claw upwards and watched the shark's skin part and open up to cloud the water with blood.

*

For what seemed like an age, there was no sound or movement on the surface; nothing but the sound of still black waters gently lapping against the cave's edge. Henry Ho and Olander looked into the black water, then up at Jo to see if she could spot anything from her position, and finally at each other.

Nothing.

Ben burst from the surface, twisting and thrashing against something, as the waters around him began to churn. The townsfolk watched eagerly from the sides of the cave, wide-eyed and slack-jawed at the struggle between man and shark. Only Ho looked on with cool composure; he'd seen this contest before, and up close too, besides, he had his position in the town to uphold.

Then the flailing and the splashing stopped. The surface of the tumultuous waters settled again. Jo looked down from her elevated vantage point. The only trace of the confrontation was a deeper shade of darkness spreading through the pool. She stared blankly at the growing cloud of red. Fresh tears rolled down her already tear-streaked face. Henry Ho and Olander floated through the aftermath, peering over the boat's side for some solid evidence of the final outcome.

Ben broke the surface of the water near the boat and gasped for air, before sinking beneath again. Moments later, he appeared again further away and flailed towards the boat. Olander aimed for him and motored in.

The residents of Sweetwater stared in disbelief, as Ben splashed towards the side of the boat and was hauled aboard by Ho and Olander. As they pulled him in, Jo could see that it wasn't an outright victory, and her heart sank. Ben's remaining right leg had been severed cleanly just below the knee. She began to sob. Olander and Ho rolled Ben on to his back and leaned over him. Blood was pumping from the fresh stump where his leg had been. Olander took off his over-shirt and twisted it into a makeshift tourniquet. He tied it around Ben's lower thigh as tightly as he could, making him moan.

Henry Ho leaned in close to Ben's coughing, ghostly-white face. Ben's eyes fluttered, as he battled to remain conscious. Ho's own eyes were now wide and awestruck. He looked like a man who'd just rediscovered his faith.

"You did it," he said. "You're the first...the only."

Ben tried to speak, but the words seemed to fail on his lips. Ho turned his head and leaned in closer still.

Nothing.

Then Ho slowly dropped his gaze to see the shark tooth-claw pressed against his throat.

"Cut her down," whispered Ben.

The two men stared at each other. Ben's eyes were clear and adamant despite his injury. Ben pushed the tooth-claw into Ho's skin, and it gave without effort. A line of warm red seeped down against Ho's throat to stain his chest. Panic flushed through the older man's features.

"Let her down into the boat!" he shouted.

Olander stared at Ho and the weapon held against his throat. He then turned the rudder and throttled forwards to place them directly underneath Jo. Ho turned to the two townsfolk manning the pulley ropes.

"Let her down easy," he called.

The two townsmen took the strain on Jo's rope and began to let it out slowly.

Ben struggled to maintain his stare with Ho. The other man's eyes were watching him closely, waiting for a moment of weakness. Jo was slowly lowered down towards the boat as it began to drift. Ben forced the tooth-claw higher against Ho's throat, as Olander reached up and guided her in. More blood streamed down the Polynesian's neck.

"Easy..." said Ben.

Ho's eyes were full of real fear now.

"Easy with her!" he shouted. "Cut her down."

Olander stared at Ben and Ho again, carefully considering his next move. He looked down at Ben's leg. It was still bleeding out, despite the tourniquet.

"I won't ask again," said Ben.

"Now!" snapped Ho.

Olander reluctantly sliced through Jo's bonds and helped her down into the boat. She immediately ripped the masking tape from her mouth and heaved a sigh of relief. She then backed away from Olander, still keeping her eyes on him. Once over by Ben and Ho, she chanced a glance down at his missing legs. Her spirits crumbled.

"Oh...Baby..."

Ben looked away, over at Olander. He twisted the claw against Ho's neck to make sure the fisherman got another good look at it.

"Take a dip," he said. "And tell them to raise the net."

Olander stared back with contempt. He started towards Ben, but Ho glared at him and snarled.

"Don't you fucking dare Bill..."

Olander halted as told and gave Ben a surly look. He then took an even longer look at the bloodied waters around them, before reluctantly climbing overboard. He surfaced several feet away, snorted and wiped his face clean with his hands. His eyes darted around the pool, as he turned around in jerky movements, hoping the shark he'd lured into the cave really was dead. He then began swimming for the side of the cave and dry land.

Ben looked at the other townsfolk and then Ho. Both men were sweating.

"Tell them," said Ben. His words were dry, and his skin was pale.

Ho looked at the townsfolk without moving his head and called to them.

"Raise the nets."

One of the men ambled over to hoist the net rope that was tied off near the sea cave's entrance, his eyes still fixed on the motorboat. He reluctantly began to pull on the rope and raise the fishing net.

Ben looked at Jo. She stared down at his now grey face with disbelief. She tried to speak.

"I...I..."

"Take us out baby," he said. "Go on. It'll be OK."

Jo took the rudder and accelerated out towards the mouth of the cave. Ho watched Ben's eyes begin to close, as he continued to lose blood and the fight to stay awake.

Ben felt Ho move. He gritted his teeth and forced his eyes open again. Ho froze. He looked down at the severed stump which was still bleeding profusely. He then looked back at Ben with a wry smile.

Ben fought to keep the other man in focus. He swallowed hard. The motorboat cut towards the growing cave mouth and the open sea beyond. Jo watched the nets there rise like some bizarre, nautical theatre curtain as they approached.

Ho continued to watch Ben closely as he ebbed away, waiting like a grinning scavenger, amused by the inevitable demise of his injured prey.

Ben's eyelids were almost closed now.

"You won't get far," said Ho.

Ben's eyes opened again, as if he was given a shot of adrenaline.

"Tell me something," said Ben. "If it's your ancestors' ritual, why didn't you ever fight for the town?"

"Me?" said Ho. "Go in there? Are you kidding?"

Ho began to laugh, almost hysterically. Ben saw the funny side and smiled too. Jo just stared at the two men as if they were both crazy.

The motorboat chugged out through the mouth of the cave as Sweetwater's townsfolk looked on from the water's edge with sullen faces. The boat finally cleared the cave and headed out on to the sea, as dusk devoured the last of the day.

Ben smiled serenely at Ho. He nodded, as his adversary's laugh slowly begin to die out. Henry Ho's face then darkened with the dawning of a terrible realization. In that moment he realized that, despite all his scheming and manipulating, he would never live to see Sweetwater rise from its watery grave and prosper again.

Ben's smile faded too. At last, the two men understood each other. He flicked the claw away from Ho, opening up the other man's throat in the process.

A hissing arc of blood sprayed into the air, as Ho grabbed his throat in surprise. He stared at Ben with bulging eyes and managed to shake his head once, then slumped forwards and slipped head-first over the side and into the ocean.

Ben sighed with relief and dropped the claw. He looked at Jo. She took his hand and held it, smiling back at him with bright, loving eyes in the half-light.

The motorboat began to rise and fall, riding further out into the choppier waters of the open sea. Jo sat at the stern. Her eyes were now fixed dead ahead, on the sun as it sank against the darkening horizon. Her expression was gentle, timeless.

Ben's eyes stared at the setting sun too. He looked as peaceful as any man could ever hope to be. He was no longer burdened by the fear and guilt that had plagued him for so long.

He was simply not afraid anymore.

Ben and Jo finally left Sweetwater; tiny figures set against the raw power of the infinite ocean and the ancient coastline that had once trapped them.

THE END